UNDERNEATH

UNDERNEATH

a novel

~

LILY HOANG

Red Hen Press | *Pasadena, CA*

Book design by Mark E. Cull

Library of Congress Cataloging-in-Publication Data

Names: Hoang, Lily K., author.
Title: Underneath : a novel / Lily Hoang.
Description: First edition. | Pasadena, CA : Red Hen Press, [2021]
Identifiers: LCCN 2021018701 (print) | LCCN 2021018702 (ebook) | ISBN 9781636280042 (trade paperback) | ISBN 9781636280059 (epub)
Subjects: LCSH: Filicide—Fiction. | Serial murders—Fiction. | Overweight Persons—Fiction. | Psychological fiction.
Classification: LCC PS3608.O18 U53 2021 (print) | LCC PS3608.O18 (ebook) | DDC 813/.6—dc23
LC record available at https://lccn.loc.gov/2021018701
LC ebook record available at https://lccn.loc.gov/2021018702

The National Endowment for the Arts, the Los Angeles County Arts Commission, the Ahmanson Foundation, the Dwight Stuart Youth Fund, the Max Factor Family Foundation, the Pasadena Tournament of Roses Foundation, the Pasadena Arts & Culture Commission and the City of Pasadena Cultural Affairs Division, the City of Los Angeles Department of Cultural Affairs, the Audrey & Sydney Irmas Charitable Foundation, the Meta & George Rosenberg Foundation, the Albert and Elaine Borchard Foundation, the Adams Family Foundation, Amazon Literary Partnership, the Sam Francis Foundation, and the Mara W. Breech Foundation partially support Red Hen Press.

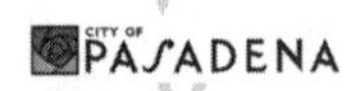

First Edition
Published by Red Hen Press
www.redhen.org

Although the particulars in this book have been fictionalized,
the murders are all very true. They happened.

CONTENTS

If I am *a wild Beast, I cannot help it. It is not my own fault.*

—Jane Austen

The slowness of revenge, like the insolence of desire, belongs to nature. There is nothing that the madness of men invents which is not either nature made manifest or nature restored.

—Michel Foucault
Madness & Civilization

FROM BEYOND

I was murdered.

My mother murdered me. It was gruesome, but there wasn't any blood. No mess was left to clean up afterward. The *how* of it doesn't matter much, neither does the *why*, not to me anyway. All that matters is that even though I'm dead, I can't go away. I'm just kind of stuck here, going around like I'm still alive, except I'm not. I'm dead. It doesn't make any sense.

Nonsense or not, here's the truth of it, cold and hard: because we were murdered, ours is a fate worse than suicide. Maybe I don't know that as fact, because I don't actually know anyone who's committed suicide here in this—I don't know what to call it, but it's not heaven and it's not hell and I never learned religion enough to say for sure, but I'm pretty sure this isn't purgatory, either. It's more just like, extension. Continuation. We the murdered continue on, right underneath the living, but we aren't alive anymore. We're just here: bodies, but not bodies, too. So far as I can tell, the living can't see or hear or feel or smell us, but sometimes, if I get close enough to Martha, I swear she can taste me. I watch as her fat face swerves with disgust, like she's just had a mouthful of nasty. It's quick, not more than a second or two, but within those too-brief moments of my mother's suffering, I feel joy. I don't feel bad about it, either, because where I am—or what I am—is a joyless place. And I don't know this as fact or anything, but I'm pretty sure I'm going to be stuck here forever. Even after Martha dies, I'll still be here. Just like all the other murder victims. There's nothing we can do about it. There's no court to appeal to or cops to call or psychiatrists to give us pills to induce amnesia or dissociation. There's no running away. This is our punishment. Because we were murdered, this is our punishment.

Included in our sentence of infinite existence is yet another joke. Once a day, every day, no matter where I am or what I'm doing, I'm transported to Martha's prison cell or wherever she happens to be and I have to watch her for an hour. The timing is precise. Sixty minutes, not a second of excess or in lack. There's no telling when in the day it'll happen, or at least we haven't figured out the pattern yet, but it always happens to each and every one of us. For one hour per day, we must watch our murderer. Early on, back when I'd only just recently died, I used to think that maybe after Martha died I might be freed. I wasn't dreaming fancy or anything. I don't mind being here in this whatever space. I just wanted to not have to look at her anymore, and maybe if the state scrambled her fat with electricity, I'd be free of her, at last, but the others have promised me that even after her death, I'll be sent to look at her grave for an hour. There is no such thing as relief. Maybe God or the Devil or Allah or Zeus is scared I'll forget who killed me. Or maybe I'm trying to force logic into a world ruled only by cruelty and spite.

Nothing makes sense.

I feel desperate for anything that resembles justice.

As a little girl, misery was a pretty good day. And then my mother killed me and now I won't even die. I still try—to die, again and often again, and every time I only meet another failure.

~

And so we are all prisoners.

We cannot be seen but we still have our bodies.

We still have our bodies but those bodies are made of nothing.

Look: you can't even see me. If you listen real hard for me, the air won't bother to move. I stopped growing the day I died, but I move through time all the same. I get smarter, sure, but why?

Nihilism is requisite and perpetual.

When we are feeling at our lowest, we embroider the details of our deaths, and as a chorus, we sing with the blackness of pitch.

We live in a fairy tale full of witches and old crones and premeditation.

We the innocent lack fairy godmothers to transform our deaths into pumpkin carriages and so Prince Charming chokes the air from our lungs and then he cums wherever he pleases.

So let me tell you a story.

I am eleven when Martha kills me.

I had known it was coming.

The terror comes in the waiting for an inevitable that has yet to arrive.

THE MAKING OF MARTHA

She puts Little Jimmy down and she stops there for a minute. Martha is admiring her beautiful son, his perfection. She is thinking about something, and she's thinking hard, taking her time with it: like, would she hear it or feel it first, those tiny bones breaking?; like, if his fingernails are sharp enough to fray the cotton of her dress; like, would he have the instinct to fight?; like, so much flesh. She wants to—but no. No, she can't.

She closes the door to my little brother's room. She closes the door to all those rushing desires, those nightmares, her fantasies. Little Jimmy is safely in his bed and nothing bad is going to happen to him and she's a good mother.

"Another one," Kenny calls.

Martha rests for a second. She puts her weight against the hallway closet and it creaks.

"Martha, you hear me?"

Nothing in the house is new. Not the furniture, not the washer, not the television, not the goddamn arguments, not even the clothes.

"Because," Kenny shouts, "I can hear you breathing all the way from here. Go get me another beer, Jesus."

Martha heaves her body forward. "Coming," she says. "I'm coming there straight away now."

~

In three days, everything will be different.

In three days, all of Martha's curiosities will be fulfilled. She will know everything she has ever wanted to know, she will be content.

In three days, Martha will put down Little Jimmy, just like she does every day, once at ten and once at a quarter to three, and three days from now, Martha will also feel tired, so very tired.

Imagination is a grand thing, but when obsession forces compulsion into action, something else comes out. It's kind of like a fight between what's imagined and what's real, like which one might taste better in the end. And for Martha, the realness of the moment will feel right, transcendent: it will feel like her very first victory. It will feel like the whole weight of her body put on top of Little Jimmy and it will feel special, like nothing she's ever felt before, and her husband will have to get the next beer himself. She will repose her body on top of his for a while. She will have herself a little nap, with her son's small body lodged between the folds of her back.

In three days' time.

No sooner and no further into the future than anyone might predict, either. But no one could've predicted this. Even after death, this story is always a surprise.

~

Martha's always been fat. When she was a little girl, the nicer ladies called her *hefty*. A *heifer*. Some people called her *healthy*, but there was nothing healthy about her. No one thought she was healthy, not really. All the kids at school called her *Marge the Barge*. Martha thought they were stupid because Marge is short for Margaret not Martha, but that didn't make the hurt feel any less hurtful.

And she hated it.

She didn't necessarily know she hated it—she was still a kid then. She only knew the effects. She didn't understand its causes. She didn't have names for emotions that swelter and boil—but she did recognize that the kids at school were mean and she was nothing better than a weak little crybaby. Some kid, maybe Debbi with her buck teeth and poodle hair, maybe it was Juan with his mean smirk and sinister eyes, maybe it was Ariel, just like the Little Mermaid, only this was long before *The Little Mermaid* was even a Disney movie, but this Ariel was just as pretty and passionate, would yell out "Marge the Barge! Marge the Barge!" and her eyes would swell up like an allergic reaction and she couldn't breathe. It hurt too much. She didn't even do anything to them. She wasn't trying to talk to them or bother them. They were just mean. For no reason except to be mean to her, and so she'd have to run to the bathroom. Or, she'd try to run to the bathroom, and for anyone else it might've been running but Martha was fat, she was a barge. She shuffled out of their sight, and her shorts went up like accordions between her thighs. She'd hide behind a stall until her eyes and nose became clear again, but she emerged splotched. She would have to return to the classroom, her pale skin mapped red to signify land, and all the other kids would watch and laugh and judge as the oceans slowly eroded the shores of her fat face until it was all white again, paler than before, and they just kept on mocking her.

It was cruel, but they were children. Children aren't innocent. Don't be fooled by their weightless eyes and laughter. Children are just young, but youth doesn't equate to not knowing any better. They know. They always know.

It wasn't just that she was fat, either. Back in the day when Martha was in elementary school here in southern New Mexico, backwoods even though there weren't any woods around, the borderlands, trashy like trash, Martha understood desire, full-bodied and hungry desire. She wasn't like the other kids around here.

As a girl, Martha knew she was something special. She was good at math and reading, had pretty blonde hair that her mama fixed into a bun at the base of her neck, and the cutest goddamn freckles.

She didn't care about what the kids at school called her. She would show them—and she would. Later, much later.

And then everything changed because of Janie McDonagall.

~

One day, in Math class, Janie McDonagall took a pair of scissors to Martha's bun, just because Martha got an A on her math quiz and Janie got a D. D minus, actually, barely a hair above failing, and worse than her embarrassment was Martha. She was gross and she was yuck and she didn't deserve to get a good grade. She didn't deserve anything.

Janie did it in stealth, in silence. She'd hidden the scissors inside her desk. It was premeditated. She'd thought about it, planned it, meticulously even. So while the teacher, Missus Rodriguez, was still handing back the math quizzes, Janie was ready.

The fact that Janie was so ready would lead anyone to recognize that she would've cut off Martha's hair no matter what—grade or not, nothing would've changed it—and motives are motives and Janie didn't need a motive, not really, for premeditation to be premeditated, but she had one, for sure: Martha's crime was her existence. She was so gross she shouldn't even be allowed to be alive. Besides, what does motive matter if the result is the end and the end is always the same? And the end repeats itself no matter the causes—in parallel worlds, worlds on taut strings, in alternative realities like mine now, in every single one—Martha always gets her hair cut off.

A or not, D or not, those grades could've belonged to either girl, really, because Janie was ready. Even if she'd gotten an A and even if Martha had been the one who got the D, Janie would've been ready in every case. She knew what kind of girl Martha was: a kiss-ass by any name is still a kiss-ass, a nerd by any name is still a nerd, and a fat fucking lesbo kiss-ass nerd freak by any name remains exactly who she is: Martha.

And so Janie slid her hand into the desk, quietly, quietly, quickly, and her slim fingers made loops around the scissors' green plastic handle.

Of course Martha didn't want to be a nerd. She liked the attention on some level. It was a new thing to her, praise, something she never learned at home. At least her teachers appreciated her. But what Martha wanted even more was to be cool. Like Janie McDonagall. She wanted boys to hold her hand even though she didn't like boys then, they were gross to her—maybe they still are, maybe they've always been—but she wanted, very badly, for them not to run away from her the minute she got within ten feet of them. She wanted them not to make fun of her. She wanted to mute their angry jabs. Boys were mean to Martha, and it's not just that they were mean. No, they were downright cruel, and it wasn't all in Martha's brain either. They *were* cruel. Like, really cruel. They didn't need to be so mean to her, she'd done nothing to deserve it, except be, and her beingness was enough to warrant anything, everything.

Earlier that morning, the very fateful day that Janie McDonagall cut off all of Martha's hair, before the first bell rang for school to begin, this one bully Francisco, who had always been and will remain for the rest of his life a total dope, ran up to Martha and punched her in the gut. It wasn't hard or anything. It was just for effect. The action in this case was less significant than its reaction. His fist's momentum sullied into Martha's manifold folds of fat. Still a schoolgirl and already too fat. It wasn't right. Francisco exaggerated his fist's ascent from the lard. It wasn't natural. It was an infection of jiggle, a convulsive wiggling, from his clenched hand up his torso and into his shoulders and head and then all the way back down, deep through his thighs and into his feet. Martha, the freak. The fat freak. No one else in school was even close to her size. She exceeded them by a score of pounds, at least, who's counting? All the while he screamed as loudly as he could, louder than the loudspeaker announcing that the students should hurry into their homeroom classes, "The barge is docking! Run for your lives!" The crowd loved it. They were uproarious. Everyone was late for homeroom that day, and Martha waddled into the bathroom, yet again, lest the other kids see her cry, yet again. Fat girls have feelings, too.

This is what I've learned watching Martha all these years: fat girls grow up to be fat murdering mothers, but even fat murdering mothers have feelings. Even when she's no longer a mother because she's killed all her babies, every single last one of them, until all that remains of her bloodline rolls through her own body and no one else's, even then, Martha's got feelings.

But no one is left behind to notice.

~

It took all of homeroom for Martha to stop crying.

She missed half of Reading, too.

By the time Math started, she was almost her normal color again.

She looked so ugly. She always looked ugly.

Crying made it worse, but only a little bit.

Sometimes I wonder how things might've been different if Janie McDonagall hadn't been so mean. Maybe if Janie had cared just a little tiny bit about her words and her actions, her behavior, maybe then everything could be fixed. There could still be babies growing into children growing into adults who have themselves some babies too, and I wonder if Little Jimmy would always be known as Little Jimmy or if he'd change it to James when he became a man. But he wouldn't, so it doesn't matter. Wondering is for dreamers, and I never sleep.

But Janie didn't care. She didn't know about Martha's endless sadness, her sorrow, and even if she knew, she still wouldn't have cared, so she stuck her bony little purple glitter-painted fingers into her desk and quietly extracted the scissors. She had this sparkling grin on her face, an affect of innocence, and everyone knew, even absentminded Missus Rodriguez must've known, that something was off, like way off, but she was taught, like all women are, especially good Mexican women, not to pry when there's nothing to be opened, so she sat back in her seat, happy, while all her sweet niños and niñas did their addition and subtraction problems.

Her hair was a wasp's nest of tangles and her glasses were unsightly on her nose. A film of chapstick shone on her skin from where she had missed her lips. Missus Rodriguez looked up all too briefly and said, "Now do your work, children. No more peeps, nada." They were angels, all of them, and she returned to her gossip magazine.

Missus Rodriguez lowered her eyes, and Janie was paying close attention. Even though she was very bad at math, she was cunning. She had smarts. She understood that one should never have witnesses, even if she's clearly the guilty one, no one should ever see. This is something Martha would learn more than a decade later. Now, however, there was only Janie and her green plastic scissors and her purple glitter-nails. She pulled one perfectly manicured finger along the clean lines of Martha's bun, just to see if she'd get a reaction and she didn't. Martha felt the finger, sure, but the yearn for touch made her embrace it. If anything, she wished it would stay with her forever.

Then, almost without thinking, almost automatically—the way one might retreat a hand from an open flame—she snapped the bun right off. One quick pump of the scissors and Janie was holding a big ball of Martha's hair, her hair that her mama would never let her cut no matter how much she'd begged.

Janie held it up, high and higher into the air, what victory.

~

Martha never wanted to wear her hair long.

Before Janie went and did it for her, she used to beg her mama Bernice—my grandmother Bernice—all the time to let her cut her hair. Her hair was always so full of knots that it could've earned a whole Girl Scouts troop worth of badges. A head full of split ends and knots.

"Mama," she said, "please let me cut my hair."

"Martha baby girl," Bernice said in response. Every single time she said the same thing. "You've got nothing."

The muted wallpaper was inconsistent and lumpy. It was old and peeling and worn thin in patches.

Bernice went on, "You're ugly and fat and you're just as dumb as a plate. Do you know how dumb a plate is?" She made her hands into a circle and her face was in the middle of it. She shook her head like she'd tasted something gross and made the plate disappear. "It's like you ain't got no brain in there at all. That's you, Martha baby. That's you." Bernice turned away from Martha. She lowered her head and her shoulders rounded over. "Please baby girl. Give me this. Give your mama this one little thing to be proud of, OK? I want to be proud of you." Bernice looked up and right at Martha. Her eyes were dolorous sequins. "Please baby girl. You got nothing. Just your hair. Please. I'm begging you. Just give me this. Give me something to be proud of."

And Martha said, "But mama, I'm not dumb. I'm not dumb at all." And Martha said, "I'm the smartest girl in my class, maybe even the whole school."

"No one gives three fucks about school smart. School smart won't get you shit. Not here, not anywhere. You're just dumb, Martha," Bernice said. "Just dumb as a goddamn plate, only at least plates are flat and pretty. You're like a pound of used bacon grease, you get me? Jesus, get out of here." She shoved Martha's face away. She had her eyes closed because she didn't want to see this monster she had made.

This was the relationship Martha had with her mama.

So the truth of it was that Martha hated her hair.

She resented it.

Because her mama loved it, without loving her.

~

On the inside, in those moments right after Janie cut off all of Martha's hair, she felt jubilant. Bully or not, Janie had metaphorically cut the strings that bound and bonded Martha to her mama. She was—*felt*—free. Inside.

But on the outside, well, that was a whole different play.

On the inside she felt a standup comedy routine, full of dirty jokes and primal laughter, but what she showed on the outside to strangers and teachers and all the kids in the school and to her family was a Shakespearean tragedy. The kind where there are no survivors and no hope.

Inside and outside were so antipodal they couldn't fit on the same earth.

Outside, Martha had to perform anger. She had to pretend the whole world was over because she understood, fully understood, that Janie had to be held accountable for her actions. Even though Martha didn't have a single friend, not even one, she knew that Janie had to show some remorse, something at all resembling an apology, or else Martha would forever and always be dismissed as weak: a loser, an easily bullied fat girl, a whaled flop, a dud. If Janie wasn't punished, her mama would be right that she was as dumb as a plate and she wasn't. She really wasn't.

~

My grandmother Bernice had good parents. Even though they hated Martha, they were honest, hardworking Catholic people. My great-grandfather worked very hard, no doubt, and his wife worked even harder at her faith. If there's a truth about my great-grandparents, it's that they were hard workers. They saved. They wanted the good life for their little Bernice, one that would make God proud. They said Martha ruined my grandmother's life, and it's true. She did.

Martha is a destroyer, a warrior, a beast.

She is the monster who doesn't even bother hiding in your closet.

~

Bernice had good parents, but she made Martha under the bleachers all the same. Isn't that just a hoot?

One day, in Algebra, Bernice passed the secretest of secret notes to Johnny Blainscoat, who she had the biggest crush on—of all time. Like during sleepless nights, she'd practice her new name: Bernice Blainscoat. She practiced her initials. She practiced in print and in cursive, for checks and the like. She had entire notebooks filled with signatures and hearts, signatures in hearts, hearts around everything. She imagined their future lives together, the way he would wake in the mornings with sleep still in his eyes and terrible breath and still she would kiss him with rapture. She imagined making him a fresh pot of coffee and squeezing oranges to make juice. She imagined their quiet evenings after supper, he'd read a book, curtailing silence to recite a particularly beautiful passage, one that might take her to the verge of tears, its elegance. She imagined the nights he'd take her out and the nice gowns he would buy her. She imagined him in a tuxedo with his hair slicked back, so handsome. She imagined the way he would curl his body around hers when they slept, his bare skin silky against her back, his cock standing high and proud against her ass. This would be their future and it would've been perfect.

He was a dreamboat, Johnny Blainscoat: tall, exceedingly handsome, articulate, and goodness gracious he even played soccer. He was the goalie, of course, state champion and MVP for three years running and just a stud.

The only problem was that he never got the note because Joey Barrera got it first.

It was neither Johnny Blainscoat's fault, nor was it Joey Barrera's fault.

Bernice, being so clever, had folded the note first in half and then diagonally and then in half again and then diagonally again. Then, she tucked some mysterious flap that manifested from nowhere like magic to secure the note into a pretty triangular pocket, and on the top of it, in an attempt to be extra clever, she wrote, "To JB. From BJ." Because that was her name—is, still—Bernice Jelinski.

It was an easy mistake, especially because Joey sat two seats away from Bernice to the left, whereas Johnny sat five seats to her left and three back, and so it only made sense that when she passed the note behind her, it reached another boy first. Another boy with the initials "JB" got the note and thought it was for him. How could he not? It was addressed to him after all. He thought it was fate. Destiny and fate can make such simple mistakes, so when they make one, it may as well be bold—and underlined and italicized.

Bernice didn't like Joey and certainly had no attraction to him. Despite his fair skin, he was, for one, a Mexican, and she could never have a half-breed baby, no way. Bernice wanted a baby girl. She'd always wanted one. And she'd always wanted that baby girl to be pretty and blonde, just like her, with skin as pale as paper.

Her letter detailed the many things she wanted to do with Johnny, to him and with him, whom she addressed as either "J" or "you," both of which aptly applied to both Johnny and Joey, and the letter itself? She'd composed it over the course of two weeks in Biology, drafted it many times in Social Studies, correcting this and that, moving over a comma one space just for looks and then removing it entirely. She borrowed from the most pornographic books she could find at the public library. The letter was hot, very.

Joey desired her instantly and without regret.

Any sixteen year old boy would've.

Something as blunt as, "Want a BJ?" and he probably would've risen, shall we say, to stake a flag on her virginity, to claim it as his victory. But her letter wasn't so indiscreet. It was written in cursive without a single error. It was lyrical and warm and honest. And dirty. It was very dirty.

At the appointed time, Bernice made herself available under the bleachers in the gym, a location she had devised herself. There was no need for romance or memories. Bernice didn't need sentimentalities. She just wanted a baby, Johnny's baby to be precise. It was an old gym, even back then, way back in the day, built decades before without any renovations or repairs. The bleachers had been replaced once, but no one bothered refinishing—or even cleaning—the area beneath it. It was damp and littered. Mold and moss were everywhere. It stank of discarded sex.

Bernice had put on cherry lip gloss and brushed her hair until it floated and she wore a fluffy skirt with little blue eyelets embroidered into the flowers, daffodils without fragrance. Below all that sweetness, however, she wore a black thong, silk, with fine lace trim, and she smiled when she felt her pubic hair sift along its edges. She thought it was sexy and it was. Her pale skin was luminous against the blackness of her panties, hiding her virgin cunt, anxious and still obscure.

But, of course, Johnny didn't show.

Joey did. Joseph Fernandez Barrera did, and he was about to become a man.

He navigated his way under the bleachers like a hero, and upon seeing her all made up like that, he sprang the cruelest hard-on he'd ever had. "Hey," he said. He was immediately angry at his own banality, wishing he could've come up with anything more clever, more alluring, more magnetic.

"What are you doing here? You've gotta go. Now." Bernice stomped her foot onto the ground, hard.

"What am I doing here?" He became flustered, shot a hand up to his hair and smoothed it down to cover his embarrassed eyes. It was too dark to see, but that didn't matter. "You invited me!"

The ground was an unfinished cement. Pacing back and forth, twice he'd stepped on something with the unmistakable slippery texture of a rubber with viscous semen sealed inside, but he didn't have the temper or inclination to look down, to verify if they were indeed miniature aquariums of other boys' completed desire. He didn't allow his eyes to focus on his own inexperience in this situation, which was great, to be sure.

Bernice came to epiphany slowly, but at least she arrived. "My note," she muttered. "Yes." And just as quickly as she understood, she decided, being one without sentimentalities, that Joey was just as good as Johnny Blainscoat. In the dark and the dank, a cock of any stripe is good enough to make a baby girl in her belly. That's all she's ever wanted, a little baby girl to call her own. "Right." She whipped her foot back onto the bleacher and let her hand follow her curves, from her cleavage down her belly and right on down further. She used a finger to snag the silk of her panties, pulling them aside to reveal her pink and glistening goods. "Want a taste?"

Joey dropped to his knees, dragged his way over, and not knowing any better, not knowing what he was supposed to do, put his mouth straight on her panties and bit, but gently.

Bernice didn't know what she was supposed to do either, having only read the line in some dirty book she'd scanned too quickly from the library, so she did what the women in the books did: she moaned.

"Do you like that?" he asked. His mouth was slivered with lace.

She moaned, again. This time with more vibrancy.

She laid herself flat while he awkwardly fingered her and she took his semen in her mouth. The taste was as gross as all the rot around her. And Joey, being a virgin, didn't understand the necessary lag time between orgasms. He demanded to have sex with her, like legit sex. That was, after all, what she promised. In the letter—to him.

He said, "You said I'd get more than just some easy blowjob.

He said, "You promised me everything."

And Bernice, who knows why, maybe out of some sort of misguided ethics, acquiesced. Pushed vertical against a fake brick wall underneath the bleachers in the gymnasium, standing shamefully, Bernice lost her virginity. It took him forever to cum again and he kept on losing his hard-on, and her whimpering about the pain, her tears, her lack of moaning, just gritted teeth and struggling breath, well, all that only made it more difficult. But he did, eventually, ejaculate his semen into her vagina, which may, eventually, or may not have become Martha.

~

By third period the next day, Joey wanted nothing to do with her, wouldn't hold her hand or call her his girl. He wouldn't even look her in face, declared her *the worst lay ever* and made sure everyone in school heard it.

A fly making its way to an abandoned feast might might've heard him tell strangers—the cool kids who couldn't otherwise take five minutes to bother beating him up; the drama kids who were too busy smoking cigarettes and being deep; etcetera—all about his escapades with Bernice, the tramp, the cheap ho, didn't even know how to suck him off right. A fly might've heard him call her more terrible names, too, flat-ironed lies, how she begged for it in the ass, how she was so loose up in there that he could've thrown the wide end of a Coca-Cola bottle through and scored a motherfucking touchdown. She was filthy.

And she couldn't even make him spill his load.

"Would've been better to jack off with my left hand," he said. "At least then I could've got off, if you know what I mean." He started laughing, ribbing with his new friends to laugh along with him at his super funny joke, and they did, but they didn't mean it.

Yes, Joey talked big and loud, made himself prince of the school for a day, but fast forward twenty-four hours and the cool kids still didn't like him and he still didn't matter a lick to the athletes or the cheerleaders or the drama kids or the band nerds, even the Gifted and Talented kids didn't care. He didn't matter to anyone.

One day, that's all he got.

One day of talk and then he was forgotten, more irrelevant than ever.

~

Lucky for Bernice not everyone believes every rumor that taints a teenager's lips, because not three days after she'd had sex for the very first time, Johnny Blainscoat walked right up to her in Algebra—right in the middle of a lecture about the Pythagorean theorem, which to this day Bernice finds a mystery—and asked her to meet him under the bleachers for a *real* anatomy lesson.

"I know all about anatomy." He winked. "Got an A plus if you know what I mean."

She fluttered her eyes.

Johnny leaned close, whispered into her ear, "It means I'm good at sex." He stood up tall. His eyes were shallow pools reflecting the sun. "Very good."

~

Johnny didn't stick around either, but at least he didn't make all the pomp and circumstance out of their fucking. It wouldn't have mattered to Bernice either way because even though she had the crushiest crush on him, she didn't enjoy sex with him any more than she had with Joey—and that was a *big* disappointment.

Bernice had always thought it was something one ought to enjoy, sex, and two for two, it was terrible.

The second time wasn't quite as dreadful, but it wasn't ecstasy either, and that's what she expected. That's what she wanted. She wanted to be forced into uncontrollable, uncontainable, moaning and writhing.

She wanted to be launched all the way to Venus.

Obviously, she wasn't.

Not even close.

Later, by the time Martha's in junior high, Bernice will be the most sought-after escort in the county.

Later, by the time Martha's nineteen and on her second husband Jimbo and second baby Little Jimmy, Bernice will be the most expensive whore in all of New Mexico.

Bernice always became younger and trimmer, not a wrinkle in sight. If anything, her skin firmed with age. Whereas Martha learned to accept her fate as a fat girl, a fatty, a slob, as *undesirable*—a fat girl turned fat teenager turned fat mother turned fat woman. Each progressive year just added more mass to her thighs and waist. Her breasts weighed so heavily they dragged her chest and shoulders to the ground. Not a solid five-foot-one on a good day, by high school she weighed 220. By the time she dropped out, 275. Who could ever want her? Even the desks at school inched away from her body as she approached, as if she could transfer her disease onto the objects themselves and even worse the humans who occupied them. She looked like a fat hunchback and Bernice was a hotrod.

~

Hers was a tautology of irrationality and insecurity, each begetting more of the other.

Its cycle is vicious.

~

Martha never learned love from her own mama.

Bernice wasn't a bad mother, per se.

But Bernice wasn't a good mother, either.

She took care of her daughter—her love, her love, her joy—the way any mother who always wanted a daughter would.

And to any other baby girl, any other daughter, someone who wasn't Martha, Bernice might've been a good mother, but she was cursed. They were.

~

Despite all the heartless things Bernice might've said—or didn't say, the act of withholding is often more telling and more damaging than that which is spoken straight, like the silences between words and the breaths between notes in a sonata—Martha didn't hate her. No one would've blamed her if she had, not that she had anyone on her side to rally for her. Martha's diligent devotion to such a neglectful mother might be seen as foolish. But she loved her mama something fierce, as all little girls are wont to do.

But all that changed the day Janie McDonagall cut off her hair.

The day Janie McDonagall cut off her hair, Martha learned—hate.

To hate.

How to hate.

Whom to hate: everyone, spare no one, not a soul, not a body, not family or friends or enemies.

But more importantly, she gained a new emotion: the ache for revenge.

Revenge was immune to her hate, an indiscriminating hate, a hate fueled only by feelings, a hate without thought.

Ultimately, that's what Martha's story is all about: her urge for revenge and her inability to repress it. She shoves it down and down, but up it comes again.

Martha learned that she had to provide her own justice. No one else bothered to care about her or for her. No one would sacrifice a yawn to help her.

She was all alone.

It's an unjust world Martha lives in, one where she is the perpetual victim, especially when she's guilty.

Martha will never know guilt though. She'll never accept it as her own. Not for what she did to Janie McDonagall. Not for what she did to anyone else, either.

~

Minutes move forward because that's all they know how to do. It's not their fault they are so fleeting, not their fault they cannot provide Martha rest from her hate and her anger and her need for revenge, that they cannot clone themselves into days. No, a minute remains always and forever just one lonely minute.

And Janie didn't even need a minute.

And so Martha hated, everyone and everything.

She hated teachers for making her do work.

She hated them for grading her work.

She hated them for giving her good grades.

She hated them even more when they didn't give her the most perfect grades.

She hated people for being mean.

She hated them for being nice.

But no one was ever nice to her, so she hated them twice as hard.

She hated the sun for shining and the clouds for obscuring.

She hated the rain for dropping and the sleet and the monsoons and the budding of prickly pears and azaleas.

The wind she was OK with, but only in principle, because when the winds really hit the open New Mexico valley, she hated that, too.

And it all started because of Janie McDonagall.

~

"Jesus, Kenny," Martha says, and she uses the butt end of a lighter to pop open his beer. "It's not even noon."

He grabs the beer from her and doesn't bother looking at her. He doesn't see her scowling or her wrath. Instead, he flips between porn and a documentary on aliens. He doesn't bother masturbating anymore. Sometimes, just looking for a few seconds is enough for him.

On screen, there is a wide-pan view of a cornfield and unrecognizable symbols look like they were branded into the ground. Kenny likes to watch TV on mute, so both husband and wife follow the camera as it moves closer and closer into the field.

Kenny looks toward Martha without acknowledging her face. "What?"

Now the camera is inside the cornfield, from inside the flattened corn. The camera shoots down and around and the rest of the cornfield is high with stalks of wispy blonde hair. A breeze blows through and it looks like dancing.

Kenny shakes the empty beer bottle at his wife. "I'll take another one, since you're just standing there doing nothing but staring over me anyway."

He flips to the porn. The girl has no pubic hair and she still looks like a virgin. Her face is twisted like it hurts, but her mouth looks like it's shouting delight.

He turns back to the alien show. The camera offers an aerial view, and the cornfield looks like a beautiful maze.

Martha goes back into the kitchen to bake a cake.

MARTHA SEEKS REVENGE

Martha cuts open the bag and dumps the ingredients into a mixing bowl and then goes to get Kenny his beer.

"Here," she says. She opens the top for him and goes back into the kitchen to finish making the cake. Her favorite part is cracking open the egg and watching how the whites move in relation to the yolk, how some of it wanders off and some of it remains to protect. Her least favorite part is mixing the damn thing up.

But she loves to hoist the mixing bowl over the aluminum pan and watch the batter drip down.

But no, her real favorite part is eating it.

When Martha eats, it is a feeling so luxurious that it strikes first as agony. Her tongue sizzles and her teeth thrum with sensation, and then everything begins to numb as the flavors slowly distribute themselves into ribbons of marvel. Each mastication is an ornate delight, revealing different piquancies, her tongue a palate for the revelation of newly created shades of vibrancy. She holds the food in her mouth for as long as she can tolerate it, until it nearly drools from the creases of her lips, and then she swallows. She must. There is no other way. She must and then there is panic, acute and unrelenting. Because she needs more. She needs to feel—again. In her life Martha has known only to hate and to be hated. But when she eats, new emotions bloom to life.

~

The cake is, after all, by her and for her.

It is, after all, my birthday.

Martha knows her daughter's favorite cake: chocolate on chocolate.

She knows I prefer Betty Crocker over the imitation store brand, and the same goes for icing. "Some things are worth it," I once said, tipping the cake mix into the basket.

Martha had, at the time, noted that I picked confetti with white whipped vanilla icing, but she must've forgotten about that when she was at the market this time. It was such an insignificant detail, a useless memory.

Martha sets the timer to make sure the cake doesn't burn. She sits on the sturdy chair and thinks about how big a thing must be to make those corn engravings. She wonders if aliens are the size of dinosaurs, the enormous ones.

~

It's not like Martha doesn't know that the only man she's ever really loved is dipping out on her every chance he gets. Kenny's too good for her, she knows that. He hasn't said it, not explicitly, but Martha knows that he knows it, too, and that he capitalizes on it every time a hot girl walks by. Sometimes, he'd go right up to her and ask for her number. With Martha standing right there. And the dip-head girl couldn't reckon a world where a man *this* fine would be a woman like *that*. She's such a fat sloppy dump. No, Kenny belongs in the world of the pretty and athletic, people with careers and happiness.

"That couldn't wait," she says flatly.

Kenny watches the girl's small ass flounce.

Then he looks at Martha.

He makes a noise somewhere between a balk and a sigh.

Then he flips the channel. A faint white light rushes across the dark sky. The recording repeats. This time, the light is circled in red. The image is grainy. It just looks like a star, jiving away up there in the night.

~

Little Jimmy and I belonged to different fathers, different husbands to Martha, but Kenny cared for us well enough. The tooth fairy only popped into existence if Kenny were spending the night. Then, we all moved into Kenny's house.

I only lived in a trailer my whole life. I'd never lived in a real house before, and that's how I knew something bad was about to happen. I didn't know what it'd look like or what would happen or anything. I didn't know if I'd survive it even. I just knew it was coming and fast.

~

For my birthday, Kenny gets me a microscope set.

That night at dinner, Kenny looks all happy. He can't wait to watch me tear open the wrapping paper. He wonders if I'll be careful about it or not, if I'll peel each piece of tape, if I will roll the tape into a ball between my fingers and secure it onto my palm or stick it under the table like gum. Or if I'll slaughter it like a hungry monster because the revelation of what's inside the box would be so great that I'd shred the paper in havoc and joy.

"Martha," he calls out even though she's right there at the kitchen table with us.

She goes up next to him, and he smacks her on the ass, hard. "Go get me another one." He smacks her other ass cheek. "Baby." Maybe next year he'll save up better and get me a telescope to match. He thinks about me looking into space through that little lens and all the big things I might discover one day, by telescope or by microscope, and he knows it'll all start here, with him. "Please," he says.

The wrapping paper is solid purple, imperial purple to be precise, but Kenny doesn't know or care anything about colors, but he'd wrapped the gift himself.

~

Martha met Kenny when she was twenty-two. She'd already had two babies with two different men. I was nearly six and Little Jimmy was still a baby. He's always going to be a little baby, no matter what. My mother always thought she'd bond best with me, but I wasn't like her. Not at all. I looked nothing like her. I was only bones. Martha has bones, I learned all about the human skeleton in Health class, but all anyone could see on her was secretions of excess: like margarine held solid by skin. And, although I talked to myself endlessly, Martha couldn't ever seem to talk to me, like our languages came from different families and our gestures didn't convey anything at all. It wasn't that she didn't love me—and love me very, very much—but there wasn't any bond there.

Not unlike Martha and her own mother.

When Martha met Kenny, she was already living off the State because childcare alone would've guzzled up the bulk of any paycheck she could earn and she didn't know what she could do for work anyway. She didn't get her GED and she didn't want it. She didn't care enough. Or, she did it to spite Bernice. "You're just dumb as a plate," her mother used to say. "Don't be like me. Finish high school. Get a real job. You don't want to be like me."

"I thought you was a success, Ma, right? All your money. All your men," Martha had said.

What could Bernice have said in response?

"Those men be all good to you, right? Treat you like what you are and leave you a nice big tip before they go."

Bernice looked right at her daughter. Her eyes were creamy with regret. "This is what a mother does for her daughter. You wouldn't get it. Sacrifice just ain't in you. All you know is you. All you care for is you. You got yourselves some babies, fine, but you will never be a mother."

If Bernice was a mother to Martha, Martha didn't want to be a mother at all. She hated Bernice enough to not do what she wanted, just because that's what her mama wanted her to do. Everything, in the end, was just her attempt at betrayal.

Besides, Martha didn't need some high school diploma to prove anything to anyone, least of all Bernice.

Besides, she had to drop out of school when she got pregnant with me, school policy.

Besides, she wasn't Kenny's type. For one, he had a job, like a real one. He worked at a doctor's office doing something. Martha never knew what, but she diligently washed his scrubs and hung them out to dry in the desert sun. She was sure to iron them every night and put them on a hanger by the shower so it would be convenient for him in the morning. She made a pot of coffee while he was getting ready so it would be freshest it could be. No question that she loved him and loved him desperately—because she wasn't good enough for him and there was nothing she could do about it except treat him like the best husband in the world.

And of course he was older than her, which is how she liked her men, thirty-four with a bald spot that he didn't try to hide, as if it were a sign of distinction, as if his lack of hair demanded respect. It worked on Martha, too, and lately, Martha was sure it worked on every slut on campus, not that Kenny went to the university or anything, just that he liked to kick a few back after a long day at work. "Give my head a rest," he'd say, and it took her too long to translate those words. She'd ignored all the signs, and it was mostly an enforced ignorance, one that endures.

After a while, though, she figured everything out, and nothing changed.

She didn't even bother mentioning it.

I should've been too young to understand any of this, and if anything, I should have been a better daughter and supported my mother, but Martha wasn't a mother. Kenny was my mother. Sure, our blood didn't match, but our devotions never wavered: our bonds secure.

~

Martha pushes all the chocolate icing on the top of the cake and uses a spatula to evenly distribute the gloss. Then, she covers the whole thing with chocolate sprinkles.

She hadn't bought any candles.

Didn't even think about it. Why would she?

~

Martha and Kenny met at the bowling alley that doubled as a pool hall that doubled as a metal bar. It was one of Martha's few nights out alone—one when her mother actually decided to be a grandmother and take care of Little Jimmy and me as if we were her beloved grandchildren from a make-believe daughter, someone who wasn't Martha, and in those moments of delusion, she loved us, too—and she was playing pool by herself. She looked up after sinking a shot and it was just like in the movies. There was a spotlight on Kenny and everything. Their eyes darted into each other's and it was destiny, Martha knew it.

And then a tall blonde skinny thing grabbed his crotch from behind.

Martha watched them walk away from the bar, stopping every few steps to make out and grope, but Kenny never lost eye contact with Martha. He kept his side-glance on her, whereas she openly stared at him.

After she banked the eight ball, he said, "Hey."

Martha wasn't expecting this. She hadn't even heard him come near. She had focused too much on her game that she stopped looking at its prize, just for a second, and then—poof!—there's Kenny, standing very close to her, and she said, "Hey."

~

What Martha didn't know was that she was precisely Kenny's type. Oh, for the show of it he made out like he was into bombshells—and they were most certainly into him—and for sure he cheated on Martha all the time, but it was with fat Mexican hookers in Cuidad Juarez in motels that rent by the hour.

Because he was cheap, he rarely fucked them.

Blow jobs cost less, and he always cums in the end, in her mouth, on her face, on her tits, on her ass, in her hair. Doesn't matter because it's all just plain satisfaction and then he pays them for a job well done.

~

After our dinner of no-name frozen chicken nuggets and frozen French fries and frozen broccoli, all microwaved to perfection, except for the fries, which were still icy in the middle, Martha turns off all the lights and brings out the cake. She flips on the lights and they all sing the birthday song and I start crying. That's how moved I am. Last year, Martha had forgotten about my birthday and none of my friends knew so I kicked it with them for a few hours after school and then biked back to the trailer. I knew Martha would be passed out and Little Jimmy would be crying, and that's exactly how it was.

Martha says, "Happy birthday," kisses me on the forehead, and places the cake in front of me. The chocolate is so dark that the color itself fills my mouth with shadowy bile.

"Your favorite, Arlene," she says. She says, "Who knows you better than your mama?"

The laces of my shoes are tied too tightly. All of my bones feel tender.

Martha pushes my shoulder. "You deaf, girl? Answer me."

"You, Mama. You know me best."

"That's all you got to say?"

"I'm sorry, ma'am. Thank you." I make my best smile. "I love it."

She pushes my shoulder again. Harder this time.

"It's the best cake ever," I say. "Thank you. I'm sorry. Thank you."

Martha goes over and hugs Kenny. "She's a little brat is what she is. You go spoiling her all the time and now she done forgot all the manners I learned her when she was little."

"Let's just have a nice night, can't we?" asks Kenny.

I plunge my fork into the cake. It tastes like wickedness and the flavor sticks in my mouth until morning, no matter how hard I scrub, no matter how much blood I spit out into the sink.

~

Kenny hands me a wrapped box while Martha eats her cake.

I'd never gotten a wrapped present before. I don't even know what to do with it.

I pick at the tape and remove it fatally, taking part of the paper with it. Since the paper was already torn, I claw through the rest of it to reveal a microscope set, exactly what I wanted, exactly what I've always wanted. I don't really know what it is, but it's perfect. It's the most perfect thing anyone has ever given me, in my whole life.

I hug Kenny hard, whisper, "Thank you so much," and he gives my body a little squeeze, and much more softly, I say, "I love you."

~

Kenny had sweet-talked me into watching Little Jimmy and took Martha to the Olive Garden. Not even six and caring for a two-year old: it was nothing new to me.

He put the ring inside a breadstick, and he really meant it when he asked her.

It's only later that he would regret his decision.

Not too much later, but still, later.

Later, there is only penitence.

~

After dinner, we women are clearing the table, and, "You didn't eat all your cake," Martha says. "What?" Martha looks at me fiercely. "Didn't like it or something? I made that shit for you."

I look down at the slice of cake that I've only take one bite out of—to be polite. Just for the show of it.

"You're such a little shit."

And Kenny's there all of a sudden. "Hey what's going on?" He saves the day.

"I was just going to my room is all." I put my head down to avoid Martha's eyes. I crumple up the wrapping paper and throw it into the trash. I tuck the microscope under my arm and go away.

I hate chocolate. My mother knows I hate chocolate. The cake is a punishment—but for what?

I go to the bathroom and gag, but nothing digested comes out.

~

Martha knocked on Bernice's door. They are meeting her mother for the first time. Bernice opened the door, said, "Come on in, Number Three."

"Jesus," Martha said. "Please mama be nice, can't you?"

Her voice was not sly. She wasn't trying to hide her disdain.

"OK, fine," Bernice said. She nodded her head toward the living room.

Martha and Kenny sat on the loveseat and Bernice sat across from them in the easy chair. The table was covered in ashtrays and

QVC was playing on the TV. The woman on the TV was smiling while furiously chopping something red, presumably tomatoes, and Bernice turned the channel before Martha could find out what it was for sure. Maybe they were bell peppers. Or chilies.

"Name's Kenny, ma'am," and Kenny made to stand to shake her hand.

Bernice lowered her hand to tell him to sit the fuck down. "No need for that shit," she said. She said, "We're past the need for stupid formalities, ain't we?"

Kenny finished standing up because he couldn't sit back down fast enough because an object in motion has to stay in motion. He wiped his hands on his jeans, maybe to smooth them down—why didn't he wear slacks? He's so stupid—maybe to clear off the sweat. "I work at a doctor's office, ma'am."

"I didn't ask you about that yet."

"This is fucking stupid." Bernice had put up new curtains. "You don't matter." But the wallpaper was starting to yellow at the corners. "You're a goddamn bitch, mama, you know that?" Martha could barely count the empty glass bottles, each one large and expensive. Her mama loved whiskey and gin and vodka and everything else, too. "Let's go."

And Kenny followed Martha's lead out of the door.

He knew he wasn't the first, but he didn't think it'd go down like this.

There's so much Kenny didn't know and doesn't, still.

There's so much Kenny chooses not to know, oh Kenny.

~

Outside of her mother's house that night, Martha cried so hard she nearly toppled over. Kenny had to use the whole of his core strength to keep them both upright. He lowered Martha onto a curb and listened to her litany against her mother, one so filled with violence that he was, just for a second, scared, as if he saw Martha for the first time.

And just as quickly, "There, there," and Kenny's ephemeral feeling chased after an invisible little bunny rabbit like a greyhound around an oval track. Everyone was safe for just a while longer, except for that bunny, who is dead, already so dead it's evaporated into its corpse into the air—and, "Breathe, baby." He rubbed her back and pushed her hair behind her ears and her green eyes shone like scales under such a big moon. "Breathe it out, baby. It's all going to be OK, just you wait and see, OK? Kenny's gonna make everything OK for his baby."

Twice married and twice divorced, and now there's Kenny and this time it will be different. How could all these men desire her? Kenny opened his arms to her. His body seemed underdeveloped against hers, almost juvenile.

She cannot fit between his embrace.

She had weighed herself that morning: 287 pounds. And it's always becoming more, adding, adding up, but what can she do? It's getting worse. How does he love her? How can it possibly continue and forever? But he must. She will make him. She won't let her mother have another victory, not with Kenny, not ever again.

"You're sure?" she asks.

"Babe, you know I love you."

"Promise me."

"You're being silly."

"Please?"

Her voice is no longer desperate. It is commanding. Kenny is her object of happiness. He is hers to own. He will never know freedom again.

"I promise."

~

I only found out about birthdays when I was four. Martha was showing me photographs and I pointed to one and Martha said, "That's the day you turned one. Look at you. You were so perfect then."

"But how'd you know?"

"Know what?"

"That I was one?"

"You stupid, Arlene?" Martha slammed the album shut. She swung her body forward to gain enough momentum to get off the futon. We were still living in the trailer then, and whole thing shifted underneath us.

~

Now, I don't want to open the box just as much as I want to know what's inside. Magic is in there, I know it. Magic and knowledge and everything great is inside there, but I resist and leave the box unopened.

Later, Kenny will ask me why he doesn't see me using my new microscope set and I will stumble out some obvious excuse and Kenny's feelings will be hurt and it's all because I don't want to destroy something so perfect. But how could I explain that in words clear enough for Kenny to understand? "I have math homework," I will say, and the sign on my door says, "Arlene's Room," in purple glitter bubble letters.

~

From my room, I hear a fight rev its engine. I push my fingers into my ears, but I can hear every word, even the intentionally quiet ones. Oh, a fight is nothing new for me, but this one is different. I could just feel that it is. The words are paced the same, the same script is being used, but something is wrong, and all I can do is wait to see what demons are coming forth. All I can do is wait.

~

Things weren't always this way. In this one, Martha and me and Little Jimmy were still living in the trailer, so it must've been early in their relationship. Kenny took the family to Peter Piper Pizza for dinner, and he gave me a whole twenty dollars worth of tokens. Little Jimmy was too much of a baby to play, so I got all the spoils to myself, except for this stuffed purple monkey that I won from the claw machine. I'd wanted to keep it, but I got tons of toys and fun that day and Little Jimmy got nothing. That stupid monkey would become Little Jimmy's item, his safety, for the rest of his life, but there wasn't much left to that anyway, so it doesn't matter. None of this matters, in the end.

While I was out playing in the ball pit, Martha asked, "How was your day?"

"Long," Kenny said. He yawned and stretched his arm around Martha and pulled her closer to him. "But it feels better now that I'm with you, babe."

"You know I hate it when you call me that, and don't you go pretending you ain't know what I'm talking about."

Kenny made a funny face and clownishly shrugged. Martha, too, started laughing, and even Little Jimmy in his baby seat shared in the good laugh.

A week before, I was watching the news and the anchor lady said there's been an outbreak of water moccasins in ball pits across the country. The anchor lady said to be careful. The anchor lady said the employees did it because they weren't being paid enough and when they worked a lot more hours than they were supposed to, sometimes they weren't paid anything at all.

Everyone out there was laughing, and I watched from inside the ball pit, ready for a viper to strike.

I didn't think death by snake bite was a half bad way to go. Maybe it would hurt, but maybe snake poison worked fast, I didn't know. Maybe if that had happened, I wouldn't be stuck here, caught between life and death, forced to keep on watching Martha for murdering me—and all my siblings, too.

~

Back then I had not yet learned the intimacy of death. Little Jimmy was still alive, playing with that funny purple monkey, laughing all the time, but all I could think about was the snakes in the ball pit. That night, I looked up the different types of poisonous snakes in the encyclopedia. There are only four families of snakes that are venomous: Elapidae, Viperidae, Atractaspidinae, and Colubridae.

Elapidae means something like sea-fish in Greek, and they live in the Tropics, which is not anywhere close to New Mexico. Some popular examples are the King Cobra and death adders. Their venom is something called neurotoxic and that means that whoever is bitten can't move. I don't think these were the types of snakes in the ball pit because they don't live here. Maybe someone could have bought some on vacation, but the people who work at Peter Piper Pizza probably don't go on a lot of vacations, especially because they were saying that they don't get paid enough money and vacations cost a lot. I don't really know though because I have never been on a vacation. Kenny said he would take us and I hoped I'd get to go to see the ocean one day. I've never seen an ocean, but on the map it looks really big.

Then, there are the vipers. Viper comes from the Latin word *vipera*, which is kind of like two words smashed together: *vivus*, which means living, and *parere*, which means to beget. Beget means to make babies, I think, and I think they're called vipers because they have this magic ability called viviparity, which means giving live birth. I'm not really sure what that means and the encyclopedia didn't explain it very well. Vipers have hollow fangs, and when they strike at you, it's supposed to feel more like a stab than a bite. Just because a viper bites you doesn't actually mean you'll die though because they don't always eject venom. Sometimes, they use something called a dry bite, and that's because they need to save their venom for a better time. Vipers can make as much venom as they want, but if they use it up, it takes time to make more. You can die from a viper bite because your blood pressure will collapse. I'm not too sure what that means but I think it means the poison will make your blood so heavy that it can't make it through your body anymore. It's supposed to be very painful. There are vipers that live here in New Mexico. I've never seen one, but there was a picture of the Western diamondback rattlesnake in the encyclopedia. When I was close by the ball pit, I couldn't hear any rattles, so even though they live here, that's probably not the type of snake that was there. Baby rattlesnakes are way more dangerous than adult ones because they don't know what they're doing yet because no one has taught them how to act properly.

The thing is that snakes just don't like to kill people. They only do it when they feel scared. They do it to protect themselves. I don't think I would ever want to kill anyone, even if it meant that they would kill me first. I wouldn't fight even. I would just let them do it.

Snakes in the Atractaspidinae family do not live here at all. They only live in Africa and the Middle East. They are very small snakes. They are so small that they usually can't even kill a grown person, but the encyclopedia says that if one bites your finger, you may as well just cut it off!

Finally, there is the Colubridae family of snakes and they are the largest family of snakes in the world. More than half of all of the known types of snakes belong to this family. Most of them are harmless. They can bite you and sure it'll hurt but it won't kill you or even make you sick. That's most of them. But some of them are really bad news. Like the ones from the genus Boiga. The Boiga are cool because they have rear-fangs, and they are also known as cat-eyed snakes. Then, there is the boomslang snake that lives in the trees of Africa. It has very big fangs in very back of its jaw and it can open its mouth up to 170° when biting. A straight line is 180° so that's really something! Their venom takes a long time to act, so even if you think you're OK, you're not. You're probably going to die. Also in Africa lives the twig snake, which is also called the bird snake or it can be called the vine snake. That's a lot of names for just one snake, and I bet the people in Africa get confused about it. Their eyes have horizontal pupils, and they see like binoculars. If one bites you, you will never ever stop bleeding and it will take a very long time for you to die and it's supposed to hurt a whole lot too. No one has made an antivenom for it yet. They can also change their color like a chameleon. Also in this family is a very special snake that only lives in Asia. It doesn't even make its own poison. It eats poisonous toads for food and then it keeps the toad's poison in its fangs!

Both venom and poison are considered toxins, but a venom requires direct delivery into the blood, like a shot the doctor gives you or a bite, of course, but a poison can be absorbed just by touching it with your skin.

To tell the truth, being bitten by a snake and dying is pretty bad, but I was killed by my mother, and I think that is probably a much worse way to die.

~

The smallest things on the inside. That's what Kenny wants me to find with the microscope.

He wants me to find all the things that make a person sick, the things that can fix us, too.

~

Nobody is laughing now and I inspect a swatch of earwax on my pinky finger.

The microscope set is a temptation. It's knowledge that I don't know that I don't know yet.

Martha screams mean things and Kenny goes even wilder back at her and everything becomes very loud.

~

In this one, Kenny brought me noodle soup in bed. "There's my girl," he said. "How's the fever?"

"I'm sorry."

"Oh, Arlene, what can you be sorry for?"

"I dunno," I said. "For being sick I guess. For being a bother."

He put his hand on my forehead and quickly lashed it back. "Too hot," he said, and then he laughed. "Almost burned me there."

"Can you leave the light on?" I asked. "I'm scared."

"Course I can," he said. "Anything else my little princess?"

"No," I said. "This is perfect."

He'd spilled some soup on the blue Care Bear on my sheets, but that one I didn't like so I didn't say anything. I just closed my eyes because they burned real bad and went on back to sleep.

~

Outside it is night and the desert sky opens itself for the stars to make themselves be seen. These glorious fires, so bright even space can't hide them.

~

Meanwhile, inside the house, the volume has been turned way up. I know the whole neighborhood can hear.

Meanwhile, inside the house, Kenny goes, "Fuck's your problem?"

And Martha goes, "Fuck you. You're a shit and so is she."

And Kenny goes, "You know what your problem is?"

And Kenny goes, "You're a rack of shit. You're a shit and your mama's a shit and the only fucking thing good about you is Arlene and Little Jimmy."

There's a star inside me, ready to burst.

And Kenny goes, "But you? Forget about you." He makes to turn around and leave but then he stops. He goes right up to Martha's face and goes, "You're a bitch. I wish I'd never—"

Martha doesn't look at him. Her eyes are fixed on a bag of flour.

"—and you stink and you're fucking gross. I mean, do you even shower? Ugh, have you even looked at yourself lately? Jesus, and do you even hear yourself talk? You hear the stupid shit that comes outta that mouth of—"

Martha measures out a cup and a half of flour, sifts in a third cup of Hershey's cocoa powder, adds a big pinch of baking soda, just a little one of salt.

"—eat and eat and eat? What am I even doing with you? I mean, Jesus, I—"

In another bowl, one and a half sticks butter, softened in the microwave, and a cup of sugar. Then, two eggs until it creams together, a medium pour of vanilla extract, and two-thirds cup sour cream.

"—shoulda known from the two men before me. I shoulda known. Your mama told me all about you. She sure as fuck did. Told me how you done ruined her life. Told me about those loser men before me. Told me I was too good for the likes—"

She adds the wet ingredients to the dry, gently mixing.

"—and you're selfish and you're stupid. You ain't even finished high school. You're useless. Can't get a job. Who's gonna hire you anyways? No one. Ain't no one in this town gonna hire you. Everyone knows you're—"

She greases two spring-form pans, delicately pours the batter in, picks up the pan and drops it flat on the counter to spread the mix out evenly.

"—the stupid one, not you. I'm the stupid one cause I'm the one who married you. Me and half this town already more like it. Don't matter. Yeah, I'm the stupid one. What was I thinking? I wasn't thinking, marrying—"

She pops it into the oven, easy.

"—mistake of my—"

Thirty minutes and like magic, it's done.

"—have to pretend, you hear me? Shit, like I can get it up for you, you gotta be kidding me. Have you looked in the goddamn mirror lately—shit, you probably don't even fit in the fucking mirror, do you? You must weigh more than 300 pounds and it's only—"

In a saucepan, six ounces semisweet chocolate broken into chunks, three-quarters stick of butter, all on low until it bubbles. Martha removes it from the heat, lets it cool; she whisks in a tablespoon of simple corn syrup, half a cup of sour cream, and one short pour of vanilla extract. She quickly whips in two and half cups of powdered sugar until it stiffens. Until it hardens. She puts it into the refrigerator to cool and set.

"—couldn't fuck you if I tried. I have to pretend you're some other bitch, you hear me? Forget about something as sweet as lovemaking, forget about it. No way. Ain't happening. Most I can do is do it in the dark so I can't see, but I can feel you, oh yes I can feel every bit of your repulsive—"

The cake cools on the rack for thirty minutes. Martha pops the spring latches and releases the two cakes. She spoons a thick layer of icing and spreads it out. She lays one cake atop the other and slathers more icing everywhere. It's green and very creamy.

"—and you know, thank fucking God I ain't have no kids with you. It'd be better for those kids if you just died cause even the State'd take better to them than—"

Martha eats the cake right there, standing over the stove. The oven's still going so it's warm on her belly. It makes her sweat. She doesn't look at Kenny. She doesn't bother dividing it into slices, just fork after fork into and out of—

"—your mouth, your crude and ugly and stupid mouth. What have I done with my life? What have you done to me?"

And on and on he goes.

"You're such a selfish bitch. That's what you are."

He sacks town after town, burning everything along the way, insult after insult, right on the sweet spot.

He goes on like that for hours. Martha never looks at him. Her face is serene, contemplative, baking cake after cake, making each one disappear into her crude and ugly and stupid mouth. Kenny pauses sometimes like he's about to let up, but then he just starts going again. He's an object in motion, and nothing wants to stop him.

She is the culprit.

She is to blame.

Everything is because of her.

She's a pig, a cunt, and who is she to disagree? Who is she to say he's wrong?

Martha never speaks, says not a single word. No sound comes from her mouth, except chewing and swallowing, chewing and swallowing. Yes, she is swallowing everything Kenny is saying, every last crumb. Her eyes are composed. She is looking away to a distant land, to a time long, long ago.

~

Meanwhile, Jupiter is out tonight. Jupiter, I learned in school, is huge. I know all about the planets, like how Jupiter's gravitational field is what protects the Earth from meteors and comets.

Even if I were outside tonight, looking up at the sky, I doubt I'd be able to tell Jupiter from any other ordinary thing sparkling way up there.

I wonder if their shouting can be heard from the moon or any of the stars or the sun or if it's only the neighbors who will be woken and disturbed.

~

And then, in an instant, everything changes.
A door is slammed.
An engine turns over.
The suddenness of quiet: its reckoning.

~

Just another lonely birthday for me.

~

In the morning, Kenny takes a shower but Martha hasn't bothered to set out his scrubs and the coffee in the pot is tepid and too strong.

Martha is frying bacon in the microwave.

"Babe," Kenny says. His hair is still wet. "You know I'm sorry."

Martha turns to him, crying, and says, "I know."

She opens her arms to her husband and he falls into her.

He nestles his face into the cotton of her housedress. It smells exactly like her, the woman that he loves.

~

Three days later, Martha just can't help it anymore.

She puts Little Jimmy down for a nap, and suddenly, Martha feels tired, too. Maybe she should take herself a little snooze.

She lifts herself onto the bed.

She cuddles around Little Jimmy. Her love, her love. He smiles and grabs his feet. Her joy. He laughs that laugh of his and puts his purple monkey into his mouth.

So Martha adjusts herself.

By placing her body on top of his.

And she rolls, back and forth and back again, until he is dead.

MARTHA, CONFINED

Mothers are not always cruel to their daughters, and Bernice once told a story to Martha and Martha told me one too, my butterfly lids flitting into sleep.

~

"Once upon a time," telephoning down the generations, matrilineal imagination.

~

How to understand femininity, one story at a time.

~

Variations on a theme: of abandonment and hope, of a happiness that blinds.

~

"Once upon a time," had said Bernice to Martha. Martha was living in her grandparents' attic then, and the ceilings fell sharply down at an angle.

"Once upon a time," said Martha to me. We're almost a family. Kenny's snoring in the living room.

When the house is full of screaming, "Once a upon a time," I say to Little Jimmy. He coos because he is still alive. Martha has not yet killed him.

~

Bernice had said, "There was a beautiful girl and she was a princess, only no one knew it because it was a secret. She didn't want anyone to know. She wanted to be just anybody else, except that she was so pretty that everyone said she was the prettiest in the whole kingdom."

"Did she know she was pretty?" Martha had asked.

"Of course she did."

"But, what if the princess isn't pretty? What happens if she's ugly and fat?"

"Shush up," Bernice said. "All princesses are pretty. None of them are ugly or fat."

"None of them?" Martha asked.

"Not even one," her mother said in response.

~

Martha said to me, "There was an old woman that everyone hated because they called her a witch because that's what she was."

"Is this a scary one, mama?" I asked. "I don't like the scary ones."

"Shush up and listen," she said. She turned off the lamp beside my bed and the whole room became a shadow.

I pulled myself closer to Martha.

She said, "But she wasn't a bad witch, not really. It's just that everyone thought she was that way, but she wasn't. Or she didn't want to be. She even grew pretty flowers in her garden to share with all the people but no one would get close enough to see so she closed off the garden so no one could go in.

"Then one morning she noticed a whole patch of flowers were missing. She didn't think nothing of it, but then the next morning, another patch went gone too."

"Who took it?"

"Shut it. I'm gonna tell if you just wait. Jesus, you got no manners, girl. You got no manners at all."

"I'm sorry mama."

"Just listen cause then the next night she didn't go to sleep. She was gonna find out who done run off with her flowers. They were real pretty ones. You'd like them. They're called rampions, the flowers, but most people know them as rapunzels and they look like upside-down purple spiders."

"Oh I know this one!"

"Damn it, girl. If I gotta tell you just one more time to shut it, you're gonna be real sorry."

"I'm sorry."

"So the old woman was waiting behind a large pecan tree and then she saw the thief. He was wearing all black and he looked like a leopard on the hunt. He opened up the sack he had slung on his back and pulled up as many flowers as he could and threw them in there.

"The old woman got pissed like she's never been pissed before."

~

"I gotta warn you," I say to Little Jimmy. "This one is only a little bit scary."

Little Jimmy stuffs his monkey's tail into his mouth. He reaches for his feet with his free hand.

"There's a real pretty lady named Maria. She had black hair and powerful eyes. People said her eyes were like nets because she could catch anybody with them."

Little Jimmy is wearing overalls, and I had put a stone in his pocket so he could find a treasure in there later, like a surprise.

"She ended up marrying the richest man in town, and they moved into his big house and he even had a car even though this was a long time ago. They had four babies together and they were very happy."

~

"One day it was raining," Bernice had told Martha, "and the beautiful girl was outside reading a book in an orchard nearby but she could not run fast enough to avoid the monsoon. It came down hard. Her clothes were heavy and her feet were soiled with mud. And her hair—" Bernice reached down to pet Martha's head. She let her fingers dive into a cloud of sunflower curls. "Well, her hair was just a disaster. Worse than yours baby girl. Worse than yours has ever been, if you can imagine that."

"Oh, it must've been real bad then."

Martha's room always smelled like piss. She didn't notice it after a while of being up there. It just became normal.

"Oh baby girl, you couldn't even imagine what a mess it was, because the wind was blowing all around her and the rain fell in sleeves, but by the time she reached the palace door—"

"Woah! There's a palace door? Where'd that come from?"

"Shut it. I'm getting there, OK?" Bernice said. "The princess was running toward the palace door the whole time but she didn't know it because she had to run with her eyes closed so the rain didn't make her blind. That good enough for you? There's always a palace and there's always a palace door. That's it."

"I'm sorry, mama."

"Like I was saying, by the time she got to the palace door, her hair was a swirl going straight up to the sky. No one had ever seen hair done up like that. There were butterflies and all sorts of flowers tangled up in there. It made her even more beautiful, and her skin must've just eaten up all the rain because it was glowing. Her skin looked like there was a river under it. She was so pretty."

"Was it still raining, mama?" Martha asked. "And who lives on the inside of the castle? Are they good guys or bad guys?"

Bernice slapped Martha's face.

"I'm sorry."

Martha's face became hot like a furnace. Even in the dark, it was burning.

"I'm real sorry."

Martha felt a sting in her eyes, like a thousand atomic pinches.

~

I will never tell my own children any stories.

Martha will kill me before I become a woman. I will never bleed.

~

"The witch was ready to kill the man, this thief," Martha said to me.

"Oh mama, please say she didn't!"

"Course she didn't! What kind of shit story do you think I'm telling?"

"I'm sorry."

"Good, now shut it. The witch was getting ready to kill the man with a lightning bolt she had inside her magic wand, but then the man fell onto his knees and begged her not to. He said he'd only been stealing flowers because his wife was very sick and she needed them or else she would die.

"Now the witch wasn't stupid. Not at all. She saw something in this man, something like a wager."

"What's a wager?" I asked Martha, and Martha took my hand in hers and squeezed it so hard I thought my bones might become powder. "Sorry, mama, please," I said. I said, "I'm so sorry. Please, mama, please." But I didn't cry. Not right then. Not in front of her.

And Martha said, "She said, 'All right. I'll let you go, but your wife has a baby inside her and I want it. I'll take good care of it. I've always wanted a baby girl of my own. That's what I've always wanted.' And so the man agreed and then he went away."

~

I never expected to survive. I knew mine would not be a happy ending. It would be an ending that's just an ending, nothing after, just an end. I knew this long before Little Jimmy died.

Because even back then, I understood my mother's lack of self-control, her wrath. I knew there was a monster masquerading as a mother.

~

"The witch collected the baby, and she loved it very much. She didn't want anybody to hurt her precious baby, who she named Rampion after the flower, so she made a high tower appear out of a pile of rocks and she put Rampion in there to keep her safe."

~

I didn't think my ending would last forever, but it does. It's an end that just continues forever—without purpose, without story.

~

"One day Maria and her husband got into a bad fight."

Martha, yelling at Kenny again.

Kenny, throwing it all right back at her.

~

"Every day at noon, the witch would call for Rampion to let down her hair, and she'd climb up it and bring her a chicken sandwich for lunch and some casserole for dinner.

"They were a happy family," Martha said to me. "There wasn't anything wrong. The witch was real nice to the girl. She was a good mama to her."

~

Late at night, after Bernice and her grandparents had already gone to sleep, Martha would uncoil her bun. "I'm strong enough," she said to the moon outside, "but you have to come save me. Please."

~

Bernice said, "It took the princess a long time to get to the castle because it was raining the whole time."

"Why didn't she just—"

"What'd I tell you? Fuck's wrong with you? You stupid or something?"

Martha pulled the comforter over her face.

Bernice swiped it back.

Martha was crying, and her mama softened.

"The crown prince and his mama just happened to be home. See, the queen was ready for her one and only son to get married, but it wasn't like he could just go marrying anyone. She had to be worthy. She had to be special. Princesses sailed through the seas and others clopped in their horse carriages across many lands, but the queen didn't think any of them were good enough. They'd been looking for a long time, and the king was getting tired of this whole thing, but he wasn't one to cross his wife.

"And then here comes our princess, knocking on the palace door.

"She was totally drenched, but when she curtsied before the queen and the prince, a silver halo glowed all around her. The mother and her son had to hold up a hand to shield their eyes from such a genuine marvel."

~

"Save me," she whispered.

~

"The fight was the worst one they'd ever had, and Maria's husband was so mad he went away.

"Maria cried all night but he didn't come back."

Little Jimmy grabs my pinky finger and puts it in his mouth. He's teething and grumpy. It feels like there are knives coming out from his gums.

~

"They take the princess into a bedroom that's going to be hers for the night, and everything in the room is made of gold. The princess has a nice room in her castle, but this one is much nicer.

"In the middle of the room is a bed, but it's not like any bed she's ever seen before. Do you want to guess what it looked it?" Bernice asked.

"No, ma'am," Martha whispered.

"That's a good girl," she said. "It was huge. The tallest bed the princess had ever seen in her whole life. It must've had fifty mattresses laid one on top of the other, and there was a gold and emerald ladder for her to climb up."

~

"She cried and she cried and she thought her husband was never going to come back again."

~

"Please," she said.

~

"Twice she lost her footing and nearly fell. The queen and her son laughed, but it wasn't mean. They weren't being bullies.

"Because the princess was a beauty, all glitter and shine, and although she struggled in her ascension up all those mattresses, her feet were miniature clouds, guiding her up without any danger, only grace.

"From down below, her dress looked like the sun."

~

Martha said to me, "The old witch wasn't bad to her, but Rampion was all alone. She never had a friend, not even one, except for the old witch whom she called mama.

"You wouldn't know anything about that though, would you, Arlene? You got all the friends anyone could want."

I pulled the sheet to cover my mouth.

"What's that?"

"No, ma'am," I said. "Sorry. I'm sorry."

"No? You ain't got friends? Shit, girl, you don't know what lonely means. But I get this girl. I get Rampion. No one gets her like I get her."

"Yes, ma'am."

"All you do is talk, Arlene. Don't know how to shut it."

"I'm sorry. I'm real sorry."

"Whatever. What was I saying?"

"Rampion. She gets lonely, just like you."

"I ain't in this story. Don't go getting confused on me," Martha said. And then Martha said, “Rampion’s got no human friends but she likes to sing to the song birds and they like to sing back. It’s real beautiful and gentle, like the wind blowing but not too hard, just perfect.

“And so this one day there’s a prince and he hears her singing and he falls in love, just like that. Doesn’t need to see her or nothing, just her singing is enough for him.

“Now that’s love, Arlene, and don’t you forget it. That’s what real love is like, just like that. Real love ain’t about looks.”

“What’s it about then?”

“One day maybe you’ll learn but maybe not, now shut your—”

“I’m sorry.”

~

How many apologies, how many times. Girls must always be sorry, they must always confess and atone. Count their sorrows, one regret at a time.

~

“She went to the river to cry,” I say to Little Jimmy, “and the Rio Grande held all her despair and kept on flowing until it reached the ocean.

“She could feel the waves, breaking across her face.”

~

“But remember this, Arlene. Listen up,” Martha said. “You can’t go hiding things from your mama. She always knows what’s up.

“Rampion got to thinking she was all smart and she was gonna trick her mama the witch, but the witch knew about the prince all along. She wanted them to meet.

“Turns out she wasn’t such a nice witch after all, because she only wanted them to meet so that they could fall in love and then you know what she did?"

"No, ma'am, I don't."

"Damn right you don't," she said. "She let the prince climb up Rampion's hair one day and when he got to the top, the witch took a pair of scissors to her daughter's hair. The prince fell all the way to the bottom of the tower. There were roses down there and they cut up his eyes until he couldn't see anything ever again.

"Then, the witch flew away and left Rampion up there all alone."

~

"She took her babies, Little Jimmy. She took all her babies down to the river, and she let it hold them, too.

"They floated in the water like fishing bobbles. Their clothes got dark in the river.

"Soon it was night, and her husband still didn't come back. She felt the deepest sadness and sang a saraband, and everything around her wept. And so she went into the river too and held her babies tight."

~

"All those mattresses," said Bernice, "but the princess couldn't get a lick of sleep. All night long, she rolled this way and that. She couldn't get comfortable. Something hard was underneath her, but she couldn't tell what it was.

"That," said Bernice, "and she was scared she'd fall off the bed!"

Martha didn't laugh the way Bernice thought she would. The girl had fallen asleep.

Bernice pinched her daughter. "I'm telling a story here. Listen up."

~

"Finally her husband came back, but he couldn't find his family anywhere," I say.

The front door slams, and I know Kenny's gone again.

"Arlene! Get in here," Martha calls.

"They're in the river, Little Jimmy. They're all in the river." I give him a fast kiss and run out to help Martha.

~

"The prince wandered off into the woods but he couldn't see anything because he was blind so he kept on walking. He walked all the way to the ocean, and then he just kept going."

"Did he die?" I asked.

"Yes," she said. "That's what happens when you try to trick a witch."

~

Little Jimmy is crying, and I go back in to change him. "It's OK, Little Jimmy, I'm right here," I say. "Maria's husband is right there, too, standing right at the river and he sees what he's done. He sees what a terrible mistake he's made."

~

"But what about Rampion?" I asked.

"She rotted in that tower until she died. It was a prison up there, and the witch never let her free."

"And what about the witch? Was she sad?"

"Course she was. She was very sad, but just then she was walking in the woods and she saw another girl, one even prettier than Rampion, so she scooped her up and flew her up to the high tower. She named her Rapunzel, and all day long she played with bones. They lived happily ever after. Now go to sleep already."

~

"They say she still walks along the river, singing late at night. Singing a song to her babies, singing them back to life."

~

"The prince and the queen are waiting for the princess in the morning. She slides down the ladder. They ask her how she slept and she didn't want to be rude so she didn't say anything was wrong. They asked her again, just to be sure, and she said, 'Like an angel.'

"They had to do it," Bernice told Martha. "She was just so pretty, they had to cut off her head.

"And as for the prince, he never got married. Turns out he's a faggot anyway. No one gets a happy ending, Martha. No one."

~

"Is that what she deserved, mama?"

"There is no such thing as justice. Remember that, OK? Promise me you'll remember that. The closest we can ever come is revenge."

Martha closed her eyes.

~

We fall asleep together, me and Little Jimmy. I crawl into his cradle, and together, we sleep until the sun slides our eyes with light.

FROM ABOVE, FROM MARS

All alone in her attic, Martha talks to herself because she has no one else who will listen.

Let us be quiet now.

Let us hear all the words she wants to say to all the empty air around her.

~

Mama says all princesses must be pretty, just like she is, but not like me at all. I'm not pretty. Not even a little bit. I asked Mama once if maybe one day I could be like her and she told me a story and then she told me that stories are only for pretend and they don't mean nothing but a lot of times my mama says things that aren't right or true or real. A lot of times she says things just to be mean and she never says she's sorry because she isn't. I know she's right that I'll never be pretty and I know she's right that no one in my life will ever love me but maybe she's wrong and not all stories are for pretend and maybe she's wrong and one day I can grow up and be something special, like her, not pretty like her, but I don't want to be like her at all anyway. I wish I had a daddy so I could want to be like him or maybe I just wish I could disappear like he did and never be in the world again.

My mama only told me this story once. I used to ask her all the time to tell it to me again but then she hits my face for being an ungrateful little shit and she says if I ask even one more time that she will never ever talk to me again and I don't know if she was being real or not but probably she was being real. Almost always when my mama talks to me she is not very nice but at least she talks to me sometimes and she says I need to know how lucky I am for that.

Now here is the story my mama told me just the one time. Are you ready?

Once upon a time, there was a little girl who was very rich. In Mama's version she is a princess. I don't know if she needs to be a princess or not but OK fine she is a princess too. The princess could have everything she wanted all the time. She probably looks just like Janie McDonagall because Janie is so pretty and she is also very rich. When Janie smiles, it feels like sunshine is everywhere. She never smiles at me. She only frowns at me and calls me names but everybody else does that too, even my mama and my grandmother and especially my grandfather who tells me all the time that he hates me and my grandmother says the devil lives inside me and I don't think the devil can live inside a person and I can't feel him inside me neither. When Mama told me this story, the princess had a different name, but I want to call her Janie so that's what her name is going to be now. I want to be like Janie so so much and even more than that I want her to be my friend, but Mama says there's a better chance that polar bears and penguins will move to Las Cruces! I've never had a friend before so I'm being stupid to want the prettiest girl in the whole world to be my friend. I'm always so stupid and I'm always feeling so alone and there's nothing that can help me be better. I don't know why I am not right. I asked the doctor one time if he could make me better and he told me there's nothing to fix with me but how can that be right? My mama has so many friends. They are also very mean to me, but they are nice to my mama, so it must be true that there is something wrong with me or else I would have friends too. I asked Mama once if she was my friend and she didn't say anything back. She didn't say anything back and so that means she didn't say, *No way, José*, like the other kids at school say to each other all the time when they are playing and laughing together but they never play with me or even talk to me except when they are trying to be mean and make me cry. I hate crying. It only makes everyone laugh even more and sometimes it hurts to cry. Janie doesn't cry. If I had one wish ever, it would be that Janie would never ever have to cry in her whole life. I can cry enough for the two of us. I'm so funny because Janie says she hates me all the time and all I want is for her to never be sad and I guess if that means she has to hate me, I'm OK with that but I wish that it was different. I wonder what Janie is doing right now, the real one, not the one in the story. I bet she's playing with her friends and all her toys or maybe she's swimming in her swimming pool. I don't know if she has a swimming pool because I have never gone to her house but I bet that she does and I bet it's big and it even has one of those slides and a big float to lie down on. I don't even know how to swim, and my grandmother says that I never need to learn because fat floats in the water and I am nothing but fat fat fat and besides there's nowhere around here for me to swim in anyway so it doesn't matter none.

Oh, just listen to me go! I was telling a story, wasn't I? Maybe my mama's right that I'm just as dumb as a plate because I forgot I was telling a story right now even though I love to tell stories, especially to myself because that way no one will yell at me or tell me how stupid I am or how fat or how ugly neither.

So Janie was a pretty princess who could have anything at all. All she had to do was think about it and it became true and real right in front of her. What did she wish for? Well, she wished for the prettiest dolls ever who could also talk and play and be her friends, even though she had a lot of friends already and the dolls were just like real little girls only better and they were a lot like servants to her but she always treated them like they were exactly like her and not less than her. Then she wished for two puppies and they loved her more than anything or anyone had ever loved her and that was a pretty hard task because everyone already loved Janie so much. Then she wished for a treehouse and a humongous tree for it to sit in and an elevator in the trunk so that she didn't have to go climbing ladders all day just to get to the top. Sometimes she could jump out of her treehouse and land on a fluffy cloud and it was so soft she could dream up there for hours. Janie also got to eat cookies all day long and she never even had to brush her teeth or go to the dentist and she's never had a cavity in her whole entire life. She's never had stinky breath, either. Her parents were the King and the Queen of course so they went on a lot of vacations to every kind of place Janie could imagine.

One day, Janie wished that she could go to Mars to visit it and she went all alone. This is where the story really begins.

So Janie made her wish and then just like that she was on Mars! She didn't need a spaceship or anything, all she did was wish it and then poof! She was there! On Mars! Can you believe it? Well, Janie couldn't! At first she was scared. She was on a whole different planet and boy oh boy was it different! She'd never in her whole life seen a place like it. Of course everything was red. The ground, the trees, the houses, even her clothes turned red! She thought maybe her skin would be too, but no, she looked like a glowing angel, all white when everything else was red.

And then oh my goodness the Martians came out! They also were red. Their hair was red and so was their skin and so were their clothes and even their eyes and their teeth. And are you ready for the best part? You won't even believe it. Mars is really actually the land of Marthas, like every Martian looks exactly like me! Except they're red of course and I'm not but otherwise it's true if you think about it because Mar is short version of Martha and because there are so many of me there they named the planet Mars.

And when Janie saw the Martians, she didn't feel scared too much anymore but she did all of a sudden feel bad because on Earth she was awful mean to me and now she was surrounded by all these red versions of me and she told herself in her head that when she goes back to Earth she will always be nice to me in the future but of course she didn't know if these Martians were nice or not and what if they wanted to kill her or something even worse? But then Janie wished they would be nice and she was sure that would be enough. And then Janie realized that she came all the way here and she didn't even bring a present to give them like her parents always did when they visited someone especially a friend so Janie wished for the perfect present to give these Martians but nothing happened! All the while more Martians were appearing and they started to walk toward her and Janie again wished for a present and again nothing happened and so Janie started to get all panicked and she wished for a cookie and then a pony and then some flowers and zip! Nada! Nothing! It just so happened that Janie's magical wishing power didn't seem to work on Mars. I don't know why. I'm just telling the story and this is just how the story goes, OK?

But it's all going to be fine. Don't worry. I would never let anything bad happen to Janie, not even in my stories that are make believe.

Martians, it turns out, are very smart. They knew everything about Earth and humans and they could even talk in English but they had an accent of course, kind of like how the Mexicans do who come from Mexico or the people who are from West Texas with their funny twang, but they didn't sound like Mexicans or Texans. It was a Martian accent and it sounded very pretty when they talked, kind of like music.

So then one Martian walked up to Janie and said, "Hi, my name is Martha. Well, so is hers and hers and hers and everyone else here too." She pointed to all the Martians who were standing there looking at Janie. They waved at her and she waved back. "Welcome to Mars! I hope you will like it here. What's your name and where do you come from?"

Janie of course was more than surprised to hear them talk in English and everything. She couldn't believe how lucky she was. When she went on vacations to other places with her parents the people all talked in languages that she couldn't understand like the time they went to Paris or the time they went to Cairo to look at the Pyramids and that was on Earth and now she's on Mars and wow it's amazing, she thought in her head. Janie was all busy thinking and then she realized that she hadn't even said anything yet and oh my goodness how long had it been? So she said, "Hi! My name is Janie and I come from Earth and on Earth I live in New Mexico, that's inside the United States of America, not Mexico even though Mexico is super close to where I live."

All the Marthas said at the very same time, "Hi Janie. Nice to meet you. We hope you like it here and will stay with us for some time."

And Janie said, "Thank you very much." She curtsied like her mother had taught her to do to be polite to strangers who she is supposed to show respect to. "I think Mars is super cool, and thank you for welcoming me! I would love to stay for a while, I'm not sure how long—" and this was when Janie suddenly realized that if her wishes don't come true here that maybe she would be stuck there forever! And oh my goodness she didn't have any money or anything! She only had her backpack and inside of it was only some toys and a notebook and a pencil because she liked to draw pictures of things when she got bored.

Her face must have looked a little scared because one Martian went up to her and said, "You can stay with me in my house if you want." She pointed to a red house right close to them. It was a pretty house. Not very big, but none of the houses on Mars looked very big, not at all like her palace on Earth, but it looked like a place that Janie could be happy in.

Janie went right up to the Martian whose name of course was Martha and gave her a big hug. I wonder what it would feel like to get a hug from Janie. I bet it would feel real nice. Sometimes I give myself hugs, but I don't think it feels the same way at all to get a hug from another person. When my mama hugs me, it's the best feeling ever and I wish she would do it more but then she says I'm just so stupid and selfish and I need to be more grateful that I get any hugs at all.

Back on Mars things were going pretty good for Janie. The Martians were all so nice and they played with her and taught her all of their games and she even liked the food that they ate even though it wasn't like anything she'd had before, it tasted really good. Janie didn't know how long it was that she had been living on Mars and sometimes she missed home a lot but really there was nothing that she could do so she just tried not to think about it too much.

One day she was playing with the Martha whose home she was living in and they were having fun and laughing a lot. And then Martha asked her, "On Earth do they think you are pretty or ugly?"

Janie laughed. "Everyone says I'm the prettiest little girl they've ever seen!"

And then it was Martha's turn to laugh and even though her face was still smiling, Janie could feel that there was something mean inside it.

"Why?" Janie asked.

"Well," said Martha, "you just look so funny to us. In fact, we think you're the ugliest thing we have ever seen!"

Can you believe it? Janie couldn't. But she had to! And what was she supposed to say? She couldn't think of anything. It's true that she looked different from the Martians, but all her life she has been pretty and now all of a sudden it turned out that every single Martian thought she was ugly! How could that be possible? And then she started to feel the feeling like when you are about to cry and so she closed her eyes real tight to try to stop it from happening but she was too late and then she was crying.

Martha went and hugged her real tight and said she was sorry and that she wasn't trying to be mean. "I bet you're right that on Earth, you're just the prettiest ever."

Janie tried her best to stop crying, but it's not easy to stop crying once you've started. Isn't it funny that I just said that if I had one wish it would be that Janie would never have to cry but in this story here she is crying? It's just a story. It's not real.

But do you want to know a secret?

My mama never told me this story. I'm making it all by myself.

And do you want to know another secret?

I don't really like the stories my mama tells me. I would never ever say that to her because then she would stop telling me stories and that would mean she wouldn't spend that much time with me and already she almost never spends time with me unless it's to brush my hair and that's something that I hate a whole lot but at least I get to be with my mama then.

So Janie was feeling a whole lot of feelings then. She was sad of course and then she missed home so so much and then she felt confused because how could these Martians think she's ugly when on Earth they would be the ugly ones and she is most definitely pretty and then she thought maybe if only she could look like them then everything would be OK.

After that, everything changed for Janie on Mars.

The Martians were still nice to her but she could tell they were being fake, like maybe they were really laughing at her and even hating her. She could tell. So she tried even harder to be more like them but she just looked so different and she knew they would never really love her.

Every day the Martians would invite her out to play, but she made up reasons not to and instead just stayed in bed all by herself and felt very sad. She tried to eat as much food as possible so that she could at least become fat like them, but no matter how she tried she could only be skinny. She tried to paint her skin red, but that just made her look stupid and besides she couldn't make her eyes or teeth or anything else red forever because paint washes off real easy.

Finally, one day she decided she had to ask for help. She asked Martha if she knew any way that she could go back to Earth because even though Mars was super, she missed her home.

Martha said, "But we love you here, Janie. Why do you want to leave us?"

Janie tried to explain her loneliness, but Martha just couldn't understand.

"Of course there's a way," Martha said after a long time. "I'll help you, but you will never be able to come back here and I'll miss you so so much."

"Please, pretty please," said Janie. "I'll do anything!"

"You don't have to do anything at all. It's just that if I help you, I'll have to go too, and I don't know if there's any way that I can return here."

"Oh, Martha!" Janie hugged her real hard. "Yes, you can come to Earth and stay in my castle and everything will be perfect! You'll love Earth!"

"Do you really think so?"

"I promise and we will be best friends and it'll be the best! I promise!"

"Well, I guess if you really want to leave that bad, I'll help you. Here, hold my hand and close your eyes."

Janie laced the fingers of her thin white hand with Martha's fat red fingers and closed her eyes

And when she opened them—

~

Sleep, little Martha, sleep, and may your dreams be full of adventures and friendship and love and hope.

MARTHA, IN LOVE

To understand Little Jimmy's death—all of our deaths—this is Martha in love.

Martha is always in love. No matter what kind of monster she is, the men fall in line and the children fall dead.

But all the while, she is in love.

Her love, her love: her joys.

~

What can monsters know of love?

~

Martha loves being in love. Nothing feels better than it. It's the feeling that's best of them all.

But Martha is a monster.

Riddle me that one.

~

Who are these fools who fall in love with a monster?

These men named Martha their wife. It's profane.

~

These husbands made simple mistakes, one after another, mistakes that might otherwise be forgotten, but not with Martha. Martha is always the victim—and so she murdered us, her children, for revenge, all in the spirit of justice.

HUSBAND NO. 1: ARLEN

This is in the day before cell phones and apps. This is in the day when people still used maps to navigate, the stars having been abandoned long ago.

~

Martha picks up the phone and dials for pizza. It's just Martha and Bernice now. Now that Bernice makes all her money from sex, they have their own place. They don't need to stay with her grandparents anymore. They have their own house and Martha has her own room inside it. Who knows what sucker Bernice is fucking tonight, but Martha knows the guy is rich, like filthy.

"Yeah," Martha says into the telephone. "I want some pizzas."

"Yes, ma'am. Go ahead when you're ready please."

"I need a large, no two—"

"Just one second, ma'am. I've got another call. Can you—"

"You told me to go ahead when I'm ready. I'm ready."

"I asked you to hold just one second. Didn't you hear me?" The voice stops for a minute, breathes a few times. "Did I say that out loud or did I just think I did?"

"Stop calling me ma'am."

"Apologies, ma'am, but I really gotta take this other call. Can I put you on hold? I'll be right back with you."

Abandonment is silent. It never makes a big show.

"Sorry about that ma'am. You wanted a—"

"I told you not to call me ma'am."

"I'm sorry there ma'am, but it's company policy. Gots to be polite."

"Call me Martha, and bring the pizzas yourself."

"Shit, Martha from school? Yeah, it's Arlen."

Bernice's cigarette butts are falling over and out of all the empties on the coffee table. If a crime happened here, it would be a fingerprint paradise.

"And what can I get for you?"

"Give me five large pepperoni and Italian sausage pizzas. Throw on some olives too while you're at it."

"You having a party there without me, Miss Martha?"

~

Nine months later I am born, and who knows where Arlen went. I never knew him. Martha didn't keep any pictures of him or anything, but if I had to guess, I'd say I look a lot like Martha because I, too, am hideous.

HUSBAND NO. 2: JIMBO

At least Arlen had offered something close to a proposal. Jimbo didn't care shit about shit, expected his woman in her place, where it's right for her to be.

~

"You're such a fucking loser."

Martha isn't crying but she's close, right on the dangerous edge of vulnerability, of weakness.

Martha should be showing by now, but she's so fat that she just looks normal. When Little Jimmy is born, he weighs only six pounds. What's the diff between 260 and 266? Looks the same to anyone else watching.

She's seven months along with Little Jimmy.

"Stupid bitch, I ain't got time for your shit today." Jimbo grabs his keys.

Martha knocks his hand, hard, and he drops his keys onto the parts of his feet that the flip-flops don't cover.

"What do you even do, Jimbo?"

"What do I do?" Jimbo points at his chest. Then he makes a circle with his finger so he's pointing it right at Martha. "What the fuck do you do?"

"You just sit on your ass all day long. Don't do shit."

"I make more money sitting on my ass than you do."

"Whatever," Martha says. "I get my money just fine."

"Yeah, from the government and from that whore of a mama you got. Yeah, go ahead and peacock about that shit."

"Then why you always broke?"

"You're fucking dumb, Martha," he says. "You don't get business. Money's got to go out before money can come in. It ain't hard thinking. You just not smart enough to get it."

"Don't take some astronaut to do simple math."

"That's a good one." He spits out a mean laugh. "You ain't smart enough for that shit."

"You're the stupid one." She props her hands on her hips.

"Just get the fuck out. Go back to your trash mama. I ain't want to look at your face no more."

"No."

"What'd you say?"

"I said no. I'm staying right here. Ain't going nowhere else."

"You think you're talking to me like that?"

Martha slides her hand down the front of Jimbo's sweatpants. "This is where I belong. Can't make me leave if you wanted."

"OK, I hear you." Jimbo pulls at the knot of lace and the elastic gives. His pants fall to the ground. "Open up."

"And if I don't?"

"Well if you do—"

⁓

They get married the next morning at the county clerk's office.

⁓

Two weeks later, Jimbo gets busted with a pound of Mexican dirt weed. He finds God in Narcotics Anonymous and divorces Martha quick.

Little Jimmy isn't yet born.

Jimbo's not half bad though. Even though he doesn't have to, he still throws Martha a little money here and there, for the baby.

Until there is no Little Jimmy left to support.

HUSBAND NO. 3: KENNY

Already, Kenny and Martha have met. Already, he has proposed. These stories have already been told, there's nothing new to change or add: history's stubborn and resolute stability, its stagnation muddy in what has happened and a refusal to amend itself.

~

The day of the wedding is perfect. Sunlight opens up every possibility for this day of celebration, covers the entire party with warmth, holding us tightly. I am the flower girl and no one says anything about Martha's wedding dress, which is black and way too tight. Her folds drape and turn.

Everything about the day is really quite ugly, especially when it portends a future filled with such nastiness. It's revolting, the future. It's disgusting, and everything begins here, with a march to Fate's end, with me throwing rings of white daisies and Martha stomping her way down the aisle.

She's smiling because she's happy.

Kenny's smiling because he's nervous.

I'm smiling because everyone is looking at me.

He doesn't know what's going to happen next, no one does. Not Martha, not me, definitely not Little Jimmy. And that, in the least, is something we all ought to be grateful for: our naïveté is a blessing on this day of blessings, *Amen*.

Someone is about to kiss the bride. I turn away from the contract.

This Man and his Wife run down the carpet and away.

Rice falls and bubbles rise up.

There is cracking and release.

Martha smiles and it is revolting.

AN AFTERMATH

Afterwards, Kenny says, "I'm sorry, babe. I love you." He puts his arms through Martha's arms and kisses the back of her head.

Martha says, "Oh Kenny."

~

Their apologies are empty. Babies die. My brothers and sister, and then, later, me.

Our mother rolls over our bodies with her body.

She squeezes air out of us.

She doesn't break our bones.

She doesn't need to.

We die because our hearts are not strong enough to withstand the weight of Martha, all 280 pounds of her, mounting us one by one. Five years, and all four children are torpid piles of dead.

Dead as beats.

Dead as doornails.

Without spark, without life, without futures.

Kenny is still apologizing, to this very day.

Why? Who cares. The end is always the same.

An object in motion can only stay in motion.

Planets maintain their rotations.

Stars continue to beat light against the starkness of a moonless night.

~

In death, I shrug.

Nothing new here.

History is rolling and the future is gone.

FROM BEHIND, FROM BEYOND

Today, Martha is hungry.

They're not feeding her enough. She knows it. They're being unfair, giving the other girls more food.

The guards hate her.

It's because she's fat. She knows it. They hate her because she's fat.

Everyone does.

But it's not her fault—can't they see that?

~

The sun is out today, but in southern New Mexico, the sun is always bright and high, and even though there is so much up there—many, many light years away—the heat presses down.

Soon, monsoon season will hit, and rain will plunge and the streets will flood and the people of Las Cruces will take refuge until the rain withdraws and the mosquitos come out to play. Maybe they will be lucky and a double rainbow will arch its way through the sky.

Of course, Martha doesn't know about the sun, not anymore.

Today, Martha is sleeping. In prison, there's not much else she can do.

There is only sleep and more sleep, anything to avoid the starkness of memory and regret. Martha doesn't regret though; she rejoices.

~

Today, Martha is locked up in solitary.

~

In Martha's life, love arrives with naughty and cruel companions.

Her emotions thrive like spectral rainbows and circulate. They expand. Like her body, gross.

Martha erases everything, and the indentations of a heavy hand leave valleys of sorrow deep inside her: the legacy of love in cheap silver handcuffs, her fat arms reaching to touch solace, for companionships, and then she is carted away.

When she is called a murderer, butterflies chirp inside her with the tenderness of a first kiss.

~

Today, Martha weeps. Justice stands atop a pedestal and Martha can't even climb up there for a fair trial.

~

Today, Martha shoves a skinny girl and takes her tray. There is a fight, and Martha is locked back up in solitary.

~

In solitary, there is only regret because there is no such thing as absolution.

~

Today, Martha receives a letter. She writes back, hungry as a giant for companionship.

She writes recklessly.

She writes with an honesty even she did not know she had.

~

Today, Martha laughs at her toilet. It is being funny.

~

Today, Martha misses the family she has murdered, and she feels calm.

~

Martha is composed of cells, a lot of them, but no more than you or me or anybody else, really.

Today, Martha sits in a cell. Its membrane wraps her tightly. She fills up with claustrophobia, like she is being hugged for the very first time. "Sensational," Martha says, and there is no one left to respond. Her shoulders pour over her immense body.

This is what loneliness looks like.

~

Today, Martha says, "Arlene, what are you doing eating all alone?"

"Sit down if you want."

"You little bitch, don't talk to your mama that way!"

"Ay," the woman says. "Pobricita, I ain't your girl. You no blood of mine."

Martha throws her tray on the ground. Her sticky lunch stays right on the plate, doesn't even scatter on impact.

"Here, mama," the woman says. She is crouched close to Martha.

"Let me help you." She picks up the tray and puts it on the table. "Sit. Let's have some lunch.

"Fuck you," Martha says. She eats her meal standing up, her back turned to such an ungrateful little bitch.

~

Today, the buzzer comes from the loud speaker and the gates open. The other girls in her pod hurry out, but Martha can't make herself get out of bed. She stays there under the cheap wool blanket. No one can make her do anything. She's going to stay right here.

~

Today, Martha makes a collect call home, but no one picks up. She wonders where everybody went.

~

We who are made of the same stuff as Martha—DNA, ribosomes, nuclei, etcetera—we can become monsters, too.

THE MAKING OF MARTHA

I run home after school.

The house is black.

The whole of our house is a penumbra of sorrow.

I don't yet know that Little Jimmy is dead. I don't yet know that my mother has murdered him. But I know that there's a cloak hanging over my house. It halts my breath, and I cannot breathe.

I can't breathe anymore.

Air refuses my lungs. Rejects it.

I can't breathe.

Like a weight is suspended there, pressing down slowly. Like I am falling.

This must be how Little Jimmy felt. I hope he couldn't feel a thing. Even though I don't even know he's dead, I already pray that his end is calm and full of peace.

It's as if I know the future, but I don't. Not yet, at least.

~

In this one, Martha is a child again and Janie cuts off her bun and waves it around like the American flag on the Fourth of July.

This is the day Martha begins to plan her revenge on Janie, and it has to be something good, real good.

Martha's revenge will ruin Janie's life entirely, and this is no hyperbole. No exaggeration needed. No grandstanding oration.

Martha will take a sledgehammer to Janie's glass castle, not just by physically devastating her—although she will, in fact, do this—and that might've been treacherous enough, but no, it will get a lot worse for Janie. Just watch and see.

Nine months after Janie cut off Martha's hair, she will be walking home. It will be the last day of school and Christmas break will spring into life. It will still be warm out. New Mexico's warmth doesn't heed any calendars or seasons or anything at all. It grooves to its own hot beat. The New Mexico sun is incessant and tenacious, and Janie will be wearing a prim skirt, shimmery like mother-of-pearl, slip-on sandals with her exposed toes twinkling, and a button-down frilly blouse. Its white will be pure. Janie calls this her business suit.

Janie will be all effervescence and jubilance. She will be light.

But Martha will be there, too, submerged in the shadows. Martha will be waiting. She will creep. Martha will be dressed like a villain might, all black everything. Her clothes will camouflage all that's inside her, all that evil. Her clothes will fit her personality, just like Janie's will fit hers. Janie will look like a pretty damsel, and soon enough she will be in distress. Martha in black will only be a coincidence. It will have no symbolism, but her black T-shirt will be too tight across the belly, making the cotton stretch, the cheapness of the fabric will be apparent because as the shirt stretches, white strands of elastic will show through all the darkness. It will look like, along her torso, a million stars as fine as wicked pinpricks from the most elegant spindle. And Martha will be growing, always growing, both up and out, and none of her pants will fit her anymore, so Bernice let her out of the house that morning in sweats, black, to match her shirt. It's supposed to be slimming, black, just not on Martha. My poor mother will look trashy like a trash bag, but she will not care.

With all that's to come, nothing bothers Martha anymore. Nothing will sully this day.

It's a rare thing when I feel pity on her, but watching her get dressed every day makes me weep. She doesn't deserve my empathy, but I give it to her anyway because she is my mother. She will always be my mother. And my murderer: I never forget that. I allow myself to become close to her—present Martha and past Martha and future Martha, too, they're all the same to me—but I always remember that she's a monster. She was always the monster. And now she's becoming more of a monster. Now that she is alone, it's the way she's always wanted to be.

Here is Martha, hiding behind a row of azalea bushes, and she will sneak up on Janie. Janie will be skipping and whistling. She won't know the song. She makes it up all on her own. Her pretty toes will barely touch the ground. She will be floating and happy and maybe even gloating a little. To Martha she will always be a gloater, a bully, she will always deserve what happens next. Martha will sneak up on her from behind, and Janie won't hear a thing, because she is singing and whistling a song she's made up herself, just skipping down the alley right behind her house, and it's a big house, Janie's.

Janie, unlike everyone else in Las Cruces, is not poor. She's rich, and Martha will hate this about her even more than she hates her hair being gone. Martha will never know the extent of her jealousy is born from classism, a desire to have what is not yours and can never be yours because it's way out of your league, of Martha's and mine, and it's not her fault, but this will be Janie's life. It's all Janie has ever known, it's not her fault, either.

Whereas Martha, well, Martha has only known hardship.

Even years later when her mama makes a whore of herself and they get their own house, Martha will only see her own suffering. Always the victim. She will always be the lowest common denominator, but Martha will never like math again enough to understand this.

Whereas Janie's mama applied fresh nail polish to her perfect nails every single day, to match the flavor of soda pop she wanted to drink after school and with dinner.

On her way home that day, she will be happy. She will be dreaming and delirious. She will be thinking about her grape soda pop and the fresh snickerdoodle cookies her nanny Lucia will have baked for her, from scratch, because it's the last day of school before Christmas break, but every other day Janie gets fresh cookies, too.

Janie doesn't know it, but this will be the very last day of these cookies—and she won't even get to eat them. Because she will never go home again. This is all only dreaming.

But now, she only knows skipping and song. It will be the day that marks the end of school for a whole two weeks, and it's going to be the best best best Christmas vacation ever. Like ever ever ever! Janie's daddy promised her a vacation to go skiing and she's never gone skiing before and she's invited her four bestest friends and they're going to have the best time. Like ever. Ever ever.

So Janie will not be paying attention.

Martha will sneak up on her from behind.

Martha will grab Janie's hair and give it a hard yank.

And then Janie will be on the ground. Her bone will fracture just a little along the right side of her skull. It will be barely there, a crack so fine even a single strand of hair couldn't weasel in there, but it will hurt real bad, like real real bad. There will be blood and it will mix into the dirt and the sienna will burn, a burnt sienna.

Janie will try to cry out, but she will be in shock.

She will be twisted, her body, and her pretty sunshine hair will bruise with blood.

Then, Martha will step on her right hand. The same hand Janie had used to cut off Martha's bun. Martha will jump with her full weight three times until she hears the bone bust—like chestnuts roasting and weasels popping—and Janie will be in shock. She will not even be able to beg Martha to stop.

It doesn't matter though because Martha will be an object in motion and there isn't a force in the whole wide earth that could compel her otherwise.

And then Martha, oh so patient, will pull a pinecone from her backpack, and just for a second, Martha will remember the vacation she took with Bernice a million years ago. It was bonding with her mama, and they ran away from her grandparents together but it lasted only a minute because money is money and was something they didn't have.

Martha will remember how her grandparents always hated her.

Martha will pry open Janie's recherché mouth, so small and delicate, and she will shove the whole thing in, deep and hard.

Janie will not be able to swallow it, not completely, so Martha pushes it in more, until the pinecone can barely be seen behind her carnation tongue and tiny teeth.

Hours later, the doctors will tell the McDonagalls that the damage was too severe, that nothing could be done, and her parents will get angry, wrathful. They will yell obscenities, and Janie will be laying in a hospital bed and she will never be able to speak again, forever dumb, a girl without voice.

Martha had planned more, but from nowhere an old hag appears, Old Señora Garza, who will be taking out her trash, who will see it all.

Old Señora Garza will catch Martha in the middle of her crime, and she will call the police.

Around her neck, she will have one of those distress lanyards and she will pull it.

Quietly, Señora Garza says, "God help us."

And Martha will run. She will run as full as she can run. At top speed.

Martha's not built for running, but boy will she try.

But first, she will look at Janie's jumbled body.

She will know what power feels like.

But sirens will sound.

And Martha will be in handcuffs.

How many more times, Martha? How many more times?

For forever, I hope. This is my attempt at prayer.

~

Martha ruined Janie's life, but even though there were witnesses, she never got in trouble. She had to sit in at the jail for a minute, and then nothing else happened.

Janie, on the other hand, well, her story is tragic. It is more than Martha could've wanted. It was the biggest success of Martha's life up to then. Later, she will have more successes, but as a girl, this was the best she could do, and her victory sails her high.

She does not know what happens to Janie next. She knows that nothing good can happen, but she doesn't know all the horrors. I wonder if that would change anything, but it doesn't matter. Nothing can change. What's happened is only ever that. It can never be anything else.

But it gets worse, much worse.

Because Janie's parents more or less abandon her, putting her in hospital after hospital, each one multiplying the distance between them. It was just too hard on them, seeing their daughter like that. A girl who used to be perfect, a little doll, ruined.

They put her in a home in Amherst, Virginia, and then they stop paying.

When they stop paying, Janie wanders through the woods and along the highway until she ends up in Lynchburg. She begs for food, anything.

And to remember briefly: this is the girl who used to get her nail polish changed daily. This is the girl who used to eat freshly baked cookies. This is the girl who used to sit behind Martha Jelinski in Math.

In a fantasy world, something good happens to Janie next. Something good like Janie survives and gets better. She just starts talking again and her parents want her back. They're so proud of her, this impossible recovery. But she's burned. She hates them. So she goes off into the world, strong and powerful, and makes a name for herself all on her own, as a motivational speaker. The most motivation America has ever seen, says the *New York Times*.

But that would only be lies and more lies, just fantasy, nothing more. Dreams don't happen here, not where Martha lives. Here, there is no happily ever after. Here, there is only death, and maybe Janie gets off easy, unlike me, punished forever.

In the non-fantasy world, Janie again makes it to Lynchburg and she find temporary refuge at a church and the priest there is kind. They cut her hair and she prays every day. There, she eats porridge for breakfast and crusty bread for lunch and a modest meal for dinner. There is never any dessert. Hers is a simple life, but one without want. Perhaps for the first time, she finds joy in small things.

But just as quickly there is a lightning in the storm.

There is lightning and the whole church is lit with fire.

It's warm in there, and Janie does not hear the people shouting for her to come.

Instead, she is burned until smoke eats her lungs. Until she can no longer breathe.

It's a familiar feeling to her, something like remembering.

And so Janie dies, alone, in a strange city, dreaming of purple soda and orange soda, root beer and pineapples and lemons. Lots and lots of lemons.

~

Ours is a house of death.

Soon, it will be a house of mourning.

Martha will mourn most of all.

With the loudest cries.

No one else can know sadness to the extent that she does.

The greatest despair is a mother's love, lost.

~

Not a single light is on. The house is lamenting, but for what? I don't need to know.

It is midday and bright. The sun is always too hot.

But there is something decidedly black about our house. The whole house is shadowed, shrouded, masqueraded.

It wears all black.

Empty.

Unoccupied.

Not Martha.

Not Little Jimmy.

Yes, even the ghosts and monsters are gone.

And so I understand.

I run into Martha's room and crawl into the indentation in the bed where Martha always sleeps. There, I cry into the pillow. I don't know what's happened yet, but I know it's bad. It's very, very bad—and I was right.

Look at me, poor little Arlene: I was still so innocent then, so pure.

~

The night before my mother killed Little Jimmy—her one and only, her precious, her little cricket—Martha painted my nails a glittery purple, and in doing so, she was propelled backwards, navigating through this and that, until she arrived at the propitious memory of the glory of revenge, of spite and of anger, and it surprised even Martha that she felt such strong feelings about Janie McDonagall. After so much time had passed, surely some of her fury should have abated by now, what she'd done to Janie ought to have been enough.

As she painted my fingernails that sparkly glittering purple, what she ought to have felt was pity or even shame. A rosary of *mea culpa*s.

But no. The night before the day that Martha murdered Little Jimmy, her one and only, all she could think about was the sugary taste of retribution, a flashback to the succulence of producing pain, a pain that wasn't temporary, a pain that can last forever. Janie's pain was permanent, a pain without relief, the pain of a victim that will always be felt. It was a recurring tax for hurting Martha, poor Martha, poor baby girl, so fat and so lonely: it was a rapid fall.

The truth of it was that before Martha even started painting my nails, she was suffering.

Kenny's words were harsher than acid, and the holes his insults burned in her could not heal. It'd been three whole days since their fight, and he apologized, and maybe he meant it, and she was sincere in accepting, but inside, she couldn't stop the stationary bicycle churning electric sorrow. This was her life. This was her husband. Her children. Everything was a goddamn disappointment.

"Do you like the color?" I chirped.

Martha didn't respond, couldn't.

Because she hated the color. It was a stupid color, the dumbest: purple with glitter, purple with sparkles. It was stupid, stupid. Stupid, stupid.

~

In sadness Martha yells, "Oh, God, who made me this way?"

In anger Martha yells, "Oh God who made me this way."

And Martha says, "Fuck off."

~

The McDonagalls never pressed charges.

No one goes after anyone for Little Jimmy's death.

Little Jimmy, her cricket, barely two years old.

No one speaks up on his dead behalf.

No one cares to or no one even cares.

~

Kenny had been so reckless with his words, his anger, and now, *this*.

Kenny doesn't see a connection, per se, and he certainly never tells anyone at all, not another soul hears the words he chants in his head, "This is my fault. This is all my fault."

On the inside of his head, he says, "I said terrible things to Martha and now our son is dead." He chants, "This is my fault."

Kenny keeps apologizing to Martha, but she can only cry.

Her sadness is his fault. They both know it.

Kenny says, "I'm sorry."

Kenny says, "I'll never talk to you that way again."

Kenny says, "I'll never leave you, never."

Kenny says, "I love you."

Kenny says, "We have to make this work."

And Martha looks up. Her eyes are marbles. She says, "For Little Jimmy."

Kenny thinks, "I did this." Kenny says, "Yes."

~

An epiphany as much as apology: interchangeable words, ultimately, each as emptied of meaning as the previous.

~

Kenny doesn't know how to dress a baby for a coffin. He's just so small.

Martha is upset. Funeral plans fall to Kenny, but he has to work. He always has to work.

And so funeral plans fall on me.

I, too, am crushed.

~

"Will he be buried or cremated?" the funeral director asks.

"I don't know."

"This is a big decision, I know it is, but I need to know all this before we can even begin the process."

His voice sounds like sand, all crackle.

"I'm sorry," I say.

"You know," he says, "you probably shouldn't be making these kinds of decisions, Arlene. Maybe you should put your mother or Kenny on the phone."

"Burial, sir. We're going to bury Little Jimmy in the ground."

~

Sudden Infant Death Syndrome. SIDS, for short: in short, no one is to blame. This is just something that happens. The doctors explain this to us. "It's just something that happens."

Martha hollers up at God, a God who has forsaken her.

~

Little Jimmy's blood did not belong to Kenny, but that does not change the sagacity of their bond.

~

When I ask Kenny about the funeral, he tells me not to worry about the money. "Just do him right," he says.

When I ask Martha about the funeral, she says, "Get the fuck out of here. Can't you see I'm busy being sad?"

~

So great is Martha's suffering over Little Jimmy's death that she could not even make it to his funeral.

That morning, as we were adorning ourselves in the color of death, she fainted.

I had hoped she wouldn't go anyway. She would likely just get angry at me for all the decisions that shouldn't have been mine to make in the first place.

~

We are dressed all in black, and then there is no more coffin.

Before, the coffin was open and Little Jimmy didn't look like himself anymore.

Death changes a face, I guess. How could it not?

His coloration didn't match his personality at all. Everything was wrong.

Before, Kenny delivered his eulogy and his sobs echoed the church with woe.

Then, I stood at the wooden stand and said into the microphone, "Little Jimmy was the best little brother anyone could ask for." I started crying. It was too much.

I ran down the steps and into Kenny's open arms.

"I'm sorry," I said into Kenny's black suit.

"It's OK, Arlene," he said. "It's all OK."

~

The funeral, much like Martha and Kenny's wedding, is full of hens.

They peck and they gossip, because they are starving.

~

Of all the days, Martha should be here today.

For me, for Kenny.

For Little Jimmy most of all.

But he's dead already, so he does not mourn her absence.

~

When guilt poisons Kenny, he, too, begins to weep. He pulls me in closer. We are all alone. People surround us with their comfort, and we reject them.

~

Meanwhile—at home, all by herself, Martha turns up the volume and ABBA returns color to the house. Today, she is the Dancing Queen, still young and lean, just a hair over seventeen.

Martha's still young, only twenty-three, but she's not lean. She doesn't even own a scale anymore because she doesn't want to know.

Those are the wrong words anyway.

Martha twirls until she is dizzy. She falls down and the house thumps in beat.

~

I live inside a requiem.

~

So many apologies.

How many of them are real.

~

We drive away without Little Jimmy.

We stop at the dump and throw away his car seat.

~

After the funeral, the hens descend on the house as a swarm.

They waltz into Martha's home to venerate her grief, her sorrow, her suffering. There is a cloud over just this house.

But what do they know?

Nothing, nothing.

The hens say, "Oh poor Martha. You poor thing."

And the hens cluck, "He was such a perfect angel."

In chorus, "An angel."

And the hens go, "We are just so sorry for your loss."

And the hens go, cluck, cluck.

They're a sorry lot, yes they are.

They bring casseroles for Martha, for us, too—leftover ham and cornbread, tuna, enchilada, chile relleno, green bean, more variations than there are themes—and Martha loves herself some casserole.

They bring cakes and cheese and carbs and carbs and starch and sugar and sugar, saccharine like the fools they are.

This is Martha's heaven.

Hens perform scripts as prescribed, arrive in either couples or caravans to avoid being caught alone with Martha, the monster—they fusillade with the desire to gossip. Good God, they barely make it free of the front door before one says what they all yearn to say, "She's a terrible mother."

"Oh the worst."

"Can you even imagine though?"

"I bet she did it."

"I bet it's her fault."

"Goodness, the sin on your lips!"

"But she's graceless, that's for sure."

"Just plain evil."

"Even if she didn't do it, it's still her fault."

"Oh, I know."

"Yes."

"Yes."

They all agree, "Yes."
"She's a devil."
"What does Kenny see in her?"
"Oh you're so bad!"
And just as quick as that, like a snap, the hens turn all their attention to Kenny, the dreamboat. He works at the doctor's office, you know. The hens' voices drop into whispers of want, and Martha falls away from their focus, those stupid hens, useless birds.
If only—if only.

~

When we are at the funeral, Martha is at home. She's always at home, never goes out or anywhere at all, except maybe the store to buy more cake mix. When we are at the funeral, she sulks. She stomps. She jumps up and down. She is celebrating. There is so much to celebrate. Namely, time alone in her house without babies and children and husbands and Bernice. It's quiet, finally.
Martha screams out with abandon.
"Yes," Martha says. "Yes."

~

It's an addiction, the way Martha likes to watch Kenny suffer.
He self-tortures. He blames himself.
Martha wants to lick every savory swatch of guilt.
It is bright like the sun.

~

A monsoon interrupts Little Jimmy's ceremony.
His coffin sinks into the wet dirt, the mud.
Later, a double rainbow faintly glows in the sky.

~

Kenny talks to the principal and he says I can stay home for two weeks.

"Because it's hard," he says. "I can't imagine."

I don't want to be at home though. Even if I've never known an ache like this, I get dressed every morning and get on the school bus like it's any other day. I make jokes that aren't funny—I'm hiding.

~

The hens do not come forever. I am not innocent forever, either. One night, after the hens have stopped visiting but before Martha is pregnant with Erwin and then with Suzie Ann, Martha calls me into her room. "Let me brush your hair, my love," she says.

I let loose my hair, I shake it free. I offer my mother my head.

Thus begins a ritual.

~

Martha wears the crown now. She's made herself the queen.

But she always has been, always.

MARTHA SEEKS REVENGE

When the thirst for revenge turns so urgent and brutal, what sort of miracle can stop it?

An object in motion and nothing more. Without prevention. Without solution except perpetual motion.

Like a machine, revenge sprouts and buds into aching flowers, and there is no respite for killers. A murderer has no allies, no friends, is without a single confidant, and so Martha is: lonely, mostly, and she plans to kill again, two times, three times, four times a charm. Her children, her babies, little doll angels, falling down and crushed, such is the weight of her need for revenge and the expanse of her powerlessness.

Such is the weight of her body, rolling over ours.

She kills out of need, but what other choice does she have?

Who tells her to stop?

Is a mother still a mother when she has killed all her children?

Who calls her the devil? Who has such sin on their tongue?

Alcoholics have AA. Addicts have NA. There's an anonymous for every vice except murder.

For Martha, there is no staged intervention, no twelve step program. There is no sponsor and there is no relapse. There is only the continuation of an object in motion because it doesn't know how to stop.

She has no one to tell her secrets to.

And she wants to—desperately. Sometimes the need is desperate.

All Martha has ever wanted is a friend. A best friend. One who will be with her forever and ever *amen*, but even if Martha were religious, and she isn't, she couldn't go to confession and share her secrets. What would she even say?

"Forgive me Father for I have"—etcetera—"called my mother a whore because that's what she is and I cursed my husband and his name and his face, his stupid ugly face, and I rolled over my son and killed him and I lied to my neighbor because she's a dumb fuck who doesn't know anything and it was easy lying to her and I liked it but I'll never do it again, I promise, and"—etcetera—"Amen."

The kindly priest, he might call her what she is. He might be so disgusted that he can't change her from being the names of evil befitting of her.

Or, he might call her his *child*.

He might accept her blood as his blood.

He might accept her sins and forgive.

But, he has an ethical obligation, a moral one; thus he must judge her. This is his duty.

She might go to a therapist, a doctor, like Kenny said she should, but the end is the end and, in the end, emotions are dumb. That's what Martha says.

But a therapist is not a friend, and neither is a priest. They are paid to be there. They're fake. She knows it. She's not a fool. She won't accept pity.

Yes, Martha's is a lonesome life: conscience roaring against a desire so base and basic. How a dismissible, "I wish you were dead," becomes real. And easy.

It happens without punishment.

Martha doesn't *wish* to kill her children, to murder us. She doesn't wish to be a murderer at all. It's just—she has no other choice. It's like she doesn't know that killing is bad. That there are other options for her, and so she never strays from the path, follows it right along. There are wolves in the woods; she sings a gentle song.

When there are no more children left to kill, she eats herself a second slice of cake.

~

Behind her back, the hens continue to gab. They speculate and they whisper, but those hens have no imagination worth imagining. Their words are just words, like bleeding words from the mouths of lazy daybeds.

~

Words move forward like time. I grow older. Martha and Kenny make babies. Everyone will die, just like languages can become extinct. Oh, time!

~

Erwin is Kenny's choice in name.

For his middle name, Martha just can't help herself: James, after her darling of a baby, her little cricket.

During her pregnancy, there isn't a night when Martha doesn't hum nice tunes while brushing my hair. I love it. Even though my scalp burns afterwards and even though I know this tranquil interlude is only temporary—as though an object in motion can't be stopped from its motion, as though the universe doesn't grow, there can only be a pause, brief, like only a magician can do—and even though I understand that once this long moment ends, everything will follow suit, toppling into descent, but right now, I love it, right now.

I allow myself to become the fool to Martha, a joking jester, anything to elongate Martha's love: stretched thin into ribbons of sweet taffy.

~

Erwin's pregnancy was easy. Everyone hid from Martha and that made her happy. Kenny and I kept our bodies a secret. We never let ourselves be seen.

Suzie Ann's pregnancy was turmoil. Our house erupted, but when morning came, the house was just a house, once again. A new day was there. New ways to suffer, too.

~

I have never been pregnant. I will never know what that feels like. I don't care to follow Martha's head during these times. I would prefer to keep it simple.

I would prefer not to know all the things I can never know.

~

We should have been a family of six, but Little Jimmy died when we were only a family of three—no Erwin yet, no Suzie Ann.

We should have been a family of five then, and we were, for a few months.

Then we became a family of four, and then a family of three, yet again.

Just me and Martha and Kenny.

Soon enough, I, too, will die, and Kenny will leave and then it will be only Martha.

Martha will feel free.

Martha will be accused of murder.

Martha will face the chair.

Martha will be commuted to life without parole.

Martha will be commuted to life.

In the future, Martha will feel free because she will be free because our deaths are empty gestures, mere shadows of a regret that

Martha will never see. She will never see the gradients falter against all her lenticular glow. It is the glow of satisfaction.

~

When Kenny goes to work and I run off to school, Martha is all alone again and only her babies cry and she is hungry. She makes herself a cake or two, and as she pours the flour into the sifter, she feels its weight in her palm. It's familiar.

Erwin lets out a wail and Suzie Ann makes echoes that bounce from wall to wall.

It's too much.

Martha returns, not to the moment she is in with her babies and their constant complaining, but all the way back to a bed and Little Jimmy, her cricket.

The hardness of his bones under her spine.

The intersection of skin.

Suffocation.

Martha feels suffocated.

Like cotton stuffed up her nose or a pinecone down her throat.

Because—she wants.

Yearns.

She folds the paper twice over the flour sack until it is sealed.

She runs into the bedroom.

Throws the sack down.

Jumps atop it.

Martha rolls and rocks her body.

The flour is dead, but it was never alive. It's not the same thing.

Finally, the babies stop their crying.

And Martha commences, like the passing of the Olympic torch.

The oven timer dings when her cakes are finished with their baking.

One spiced with arsenic and two spiced with cinnamon.

~

Kenny says, "I love you, bunny rabbit." He kisses his little doll's head. Suzie Ann is everything he's ever wanted in a daughter, his own daughter.

Kenny says, "I love you, big guy." He tucks strands of Erwin's brown curls behind his ear. He pulls the blanket up loosely.

Kenny says, "I love you."

"Can you leave the light on?"

"You're a big enough girl now to sleep with the light off."

"But I'm scared," I say.

"Oh, baby, you don't need to be scared. Kenny's here. Kenny will always protect you from anything. Promise."

"I know, but—"

"Don't worry, Arlene. There aren't any monsters round these parts." Kenny makes like he's checking all the closets and under the bed, but that isn't what I mean and Kenny knows it.

"Please?" I say. I know what I sound like, but it's not my fault. I have every reason to be frightened.

He leaves the light on for me, but that doesn't make my sleep any easier.

~

Kenny says, "I love you," but Martha knows better than to fall for his tricks. He pulls his arms around the mass of her body, kisses her neck, romances her.

She's not going to be fooled this time though.

She's been fooled too many times now.

Too often for it even to be called foolishness. It's a flaw. A flaw is a flaw is a little fallen baby, circles of soft cotton sheets and an unmade bed. Suzie Ann doesn't have teeth yet. Not even a single one.

But this is not the moment Martha will kill Suzie Ann. Not yet. Suzie Ann can keep on living in my story for a few more anecdotes, a few more memories to be rewound. This is all I can do: delay. I can't offer her any more days or minutes, such is scorned fate. So please, mama, I'm calling you mama for this one, I'm begging you. Let us keep Suzie Ann alive, my bunny rabbit of a sister, without a single tooth in her mouth. Please, let me hold her for just a while longer.

Please, before you slay her.

Let me love her for you because you cannot.

Martha knows not how to love.

~

Martha is in the kitchen baking cakes again. Big cakes, little cakes, and a cupcake just for one. This one is special. This one is just for Erwin because he's such a special boy. He's getting big, so he gets his mama's special cake. He claps his hands and grabs the cake.

"Yum yum," Martha says.

"Yum yum," Erwin says back. He smiles and his whole mouth is covered with chocolate.

Suzie Ann begins to cry.

Martha claps along and sings a happy song to the beat.

~

Nearly three, Martha worries that Erwin may be too strong; therefore, she must weaken him.

~

I join every club and after-school sport. Anything so I don't have to go home.

~

And in rushes Kenny, just who does he think he is? He shrinks when he sees her, Martha, his wife and the mother to his children, the mother to other men's children—only one of which still lives, that's me, but not forever—and his body actually decreases in size.

He gets smaller and all he has to do is see her.

He says something about something and Martha isn't listening. She doesn't care. She says, "You hate me because I'm fat, don't you?"

"No, I never said that," Kenny says. "I love you exactly like you are, every single pound of you."

"Fuck you," she says.

And Kenny says, "I love you. I mean it."

And Kenny says, "Martha, please, you have to believe me."

And Martha says, "You've always hated me."

And Kenny goes, "No no no."

And Martha says, "I know it."

And Kenny goes, "No no no."

And Martha says, "Remember this one, you fucking loser."

And Kenny goes, "No no no."

And Martha continues, "Everything is eventually your fault."

The house is quiet for a minute.

Kenny breaks and says, "No, please no."

And Martha says, "Even the things that haven't happened yet."

And Kenny goes, "Please baby."

And Martha says, "Yes."

~

"Fussy brat," Martha says. Suzie Ann does not stop crying no matter how much she is pampered and burped and changed and fed and changed. She's nothing like Erwin. "Kenny's little bunny rabbit," she says and she smacks her baby daughter in the face until she screams.

~

I care for the babies like I am the mommy when the house rises with yeasty anger.

~

Often, I wonder where they are now, why they aren't here with me, but I think maybe they were too little and that saved them. Like maybe there is such a thing as mercy.

I miss them all the time.

This way is better though. This way, I can suffer for them.

~

"Pucker down," Kenny says to Suzie Ann, and she quiets when his fingertips sit on her eyelids. "You're just my little bunny rabbit, aren't you? Sleep little bunny rabbit, sleep."

Kenny shuts off the light and worries his way down the hall.

Tonight, Martha may let him sleep in bed with her, but he kind of hopes that she won't. He hopes she'll eject him to the couch again. This is what hope looks like to Kenny now.

The couch is the most Kenny can dream of: another night without Martha and arguing and fear. Little Jimmy was just an indication. Kenny doesn't know of what. He doesn't know what else is going to happen, but he will, in time. Oh, Kenny will learn a whole new spectrum of hurt and guilt. Martha will be sure to teach him right. I will watch, silent, and count the days until my mother will kill me, too. I don't know when, of course, but I know it's coming. A daughter always knows.

Because I am silent, I am culpable, just like Kenny, just like Bernice, just like all those stupid hens.

Martha calls me an ungrateful turd, but I feel gratitude for every moment I can still breathe.

~

The hens get ready for the great procession. This time, they will bring flowers, too.

~

And then Suzie Ann no longer feels free. No, what she feels is the opposite of free. Her baby palms push for freedom, but she's too weak or the mass on top of her is too heavy. It's swallowing her like an enormous blue whale. It's too big now, and she is a tiny peanut. She doesn't know what's happening, but the sunlight has disappeared. It's just dark all around her. Maybe it's time to go to sleep. Maybe Kenny will be in to kiss her goodnight. Everything is quiet now. It's not so bad. Suzie Ann wants to close her eyes to go to sleep because it's night time and that's when babies go to sleep. She uses all of her strength to close her eyes down against all that skin—skin that she doesn't recognize as skin, except she knows the smell. It's a smell she knows—and so she sleeps. She sleeps with her eyes still open and she sleeps and she dreams until her body rejects those pleasures with death.

~

After Suzie Ann is dead, Martha stretches her arms and legs, and her back expands over the lump of baby that remains beneath her.

She feels like a secret princess.

~

Martha is in the kitchen baking a cake when Kenny comes home. He is carrying Erwin and I follow close behind, holding Kenny's free hand. The house has an aroma of chocolate and a texture of sadness, we could all feel it. Kenny gives me the baby—even though he's not even a baby anymore, almost three, forever almost three, but that's later—and he walks into the bedroom to change his shirt.

There, he falls forward and lets his knees catch hard against the floor.

Suzie Ann is still on the bed.

It looks like she's sleeping, but he knows that she's not.

He weeps.

~

"Rare," says the coroner, "but not entirely impossible."

In his paperwork, he writes, "Sudden Infant Death Syndrome."

"Strange," he says. "Two cases in one family and so close together."

He makes a note to investigate further.

Maybe he forgets or maybe this family can only gamble to lose or maybe he's bad at his job or maybe he finds nothing at all amiss. Sometimes bad things happen.

Natural causes are just so fucking savage.

~

A fly buzzes by Martha's face. She smacks it with an open palm. "Whammy," she says. She opens up her mouth, and cackles come soaring out with the wind.

~

The hens cluck in and say to Martha, "Oh, Martha, we're so sorry for your loss."

And, "We can't even imagine."

And, "Don't blame yourself, dear."

And, "Yes, there was nothing you could've done."

And, "It was God's will, you know."

And, "She's in a better place now."

And, "With Little Jimmy."

There is scandal when his name is spoken, as if he were a sin.

Martha cannot stop weeping for long enough to respond. She can't say a thing. She heaves herself from hen to hen for sympathy. They pat her back gently, like a baby's back waiting for a burp.

Afterward, they say, "How weird."

And, "I know, right?"

And, "What are the chances?"

And, "What are the odds?"

And, "Kind of impossible."

And, "You don't say!"

And, "Absolutely impossible."

And, "I talked to my husband's friend and he's a doctor and he said no way."

And, "You don't mean—"

And, "No." And, "No." And, "No."

But nothing happens. Hens can only talk and peck.

Otherwise, they are simply useless.

~

A house of death, now more than ever: Kenny insists we move, but Martha won't allow it.

Kenny doesn't say this, but he thinks if we move, maybe babies would stop dying. Oh Kenny, you're just a dope too. There's nothing to prevent, nothing to be done.

Martha is in motion, don't you know? Can't you see?

There's nothing to stop her momentum.

The breaks must be broken. Now, there are only porcelain dolls cracking into splinters.

~

Shortly after Suzie Ann's death, Bernice leaves. "Vegas," she says, but it doesn't matter where. She could've said Paris or Sydney, it's all the same.

She leaves, again and for good this time.

Understanding daughters the way only a mama can, she balances Martha's probable responsibility against the death of her precious grandbabies, and it's too much.

She flees and never returns.

Well, she comes back, much later, after I am already dead: the last killed, the most brutal.

~

Hens come in and hens go out.

They scatter seeds, but they never root into trees.

~

Martha holds pocket aces.

~

A special cake, just for her darling baby boy Erwin. "Vroom, vroom, goes the airplane. Weeee!"

~

"If you're sad, maybe you should go to the doctor or something. There's things that can help."

"I ain't sad."

Lemon pound cake slowly rises in the oven.

"It ain't right, you like this."

"Fuck you, Kenny."

"Fuck's wrong with you anyway?"

"Fuck's wrong with me? You tell me."

It's bronze now, the cake. Almost done. Any minute now.

"Nah, I'll tell you what's wrong with me. You are. You're the problem, Kenny. Jesus, you always been the problem. Get the fuck out my face."

Kenny slams the door, rushes himself to the first whore he can find. He relieves his pain in her.

~

An hour later, here's Kenny apologizing to Martha. For what? For everything, all of it, it's all his fault. He doesn't go into detail. He doesn't need to.

~

Skin on skin, that's just romantic talk. She isn't ever naked when she murders us.

She's always wearing clothes. We never felt our mother's skin in those last moments of life, only detergent and unsoftened fiber dried in the unforgiving desert sun.

~

Martha takes Erwin to bed, and they fall asleep together. Martha goes deep into slumber and finds herself inside a dream.

It's the day of her sixth birthday, and Martha's going to have a party! All of her friends received invitations baked right into the cream-filled center of a chocolate cupcake. At least one of her friends accidentally ate the invitation, but it's OK because there was magic brewed into the mix, and if the invitation was consumed, unintentionally of course, why would anyone try to skirt an invitation to the most exclusive birthday party Las Cruces has ever seen?!, the invitee would be spellbound to walk to the nearest writing instrument and write out all the important information about the party, such as time, location, dress, décor, etcetera. Martha didn't want to leave anyone out, not even sloppy eaters, not for her *sixth* birthday party, another party maybe but the number six is unforgettable! Martha had accounted for every possible disastrous situation that might arise from her clever form of invitation.

The party would be a cake potluck, the first of its kind. Everyone was assigned a specific kind of cake to make, not buy, unless it was from a premium bakery, none of the generic cheap stuff would be accepted. Certainly, there would be absolutely no premade out-of-the-box business, not at *her* party. The invitation only said what kind of cake to bring, not all the other instructions, of course, because the only people going were Martha's *best* friends, and those closest to her already knew her so well that they wouldn't even dare.

Remember this is only a dream. Martha doesn't have friends. Not a single one. But in dreams, everything can become possible—and it can feel true.

Martha had made up some of the cakes on whim and imagination alone, combinations she thought might provide a stunning explosion of tastes to enjoy. For instance, a three-tiered vanilla bean cake with crushed guava and cream cheese icing cushioning each fluffy layer. Or, a simple chocolate cake with finely grated beets for added moisture. And then there were the normal cakes, easy cakes for the friends she found lacking in kitchen talents: lemon pound, red velvet, carrot, log, etcetera. In the note folded into the cream-filled center of the chocolate cupcakes, Martha explained that the cake would serve as gift enough to allow them admission into her party, no further gifts necessary, but, but, if her *best* friends were insistent upon it—and of course they would insist, of course they insist, surely—she wanted books, the classics, not some kiddie big-fonted, half-illustrated, abridged little girl version. No, she wanted the real deal, the kind with the removable cover and the nice smelling pages preferred, please and thank you.

Her mama Bernice had wanted to make it a surprise party, but Martha wanted them to plan it together. In this dream of this birthday party, Martha thinks back to all the fun she had with her mama getting ready for the party. They went to the mall together to pick out the coolest outfit. Her mama learned how to brew the magic potion for the invitations, and she let Martha stir the slimy liquid in the pot whenever she wanted to. She only had to ask and she could have whatever she wanted.

They were best friends, her and her mama. Well, her real best friend was Janie, but that's at school and when they play. Her realest best friend forever and forever is her mama. Best mama ever. Martha even made her a sash like a beauty queen one day in art class with glitter and puff paint.

Together, they were invincible.

These were all the things that Martha was thinking in her head while she was blindfolded. She was being led by her mama to the party. She was so excited to get there, to the party, to *her* party. Her mama had taken it on herself to do all the decorating, but she kept it a big secret from Martha. "It's gonna be worth it, baby girl," her mama had said.

"Promise?" Martha replied. And her mama tackled her with the tickles, and it was just so much fun.

"Why don't you see for yourself?" said Bernice. "Look, Martha, look."

"Wow," Martha said. She listened to her mama and had herself a look around. Martha was inside a cake-maze, with cakes stacked higher than her head! The cakes were the size of houses, although one-story ones, not two. Las Cruces has an ordinance against anything higher than three. It's an issue of cooling, you see. It's harder to chill because heat rises and swamp coolers offer only limited relief.

Her friends all grinned with excitement. Their glee is bountiful.

"But wait," said Bernice, "there's more."

Wait for it: her mama had planned this all in secret. It was a premeditated surprise!

In the middle of each cake was baked a book, a classic, bound in leather and then wrapped carefully in a thick plastic wrap, something like say, a tarp, and if she wanted to get to her present, well, she's just have to eat herself the whole cake, or at least half of it. This isn't going to be an easy challenge for a six-year old girl, but this is a task she's been training for the whole of her life.

There is a special movement between dreaming and waking. Martha has been fed cake more than vegetables her whole life, and even though she is thin and beautiful in this dream, her body knows how to eat cake and a lot of it. It's as if real life has compressed itself into her dream body, memory driven to submission—submission to desire—desire to desire, even in the deepest stages of slumber.

But Martha's not a greedy girl, no way. She wants to share all these beautiful cakes with her friends. They are all going eat eat eat! Just imagine!

Martha runs into the house, gliding on a pavement made of ice cream—a rocky road? Haha!—to gather enough large spoons to fit every single mouth.

Except—

Except—

Inside the house, she finds that the whole kitchen has been lined with plastic tarp, and suddenly she is no longer lithe and skating. Now she's Herculean in size and in task. Each step crinkles the plastic, and the plastic sticks to her sticky ice cream feet. She should've just eaten the cakes herself. She should've been parsimonious with her gifts. They are, after all, for her: for Martha and only Martha. She has no *obligation* to these people. No one told her she has to share. No one would've judged her. It's her birthday! No one ever taught her altruism. It's just a word she found in the dictionary and it felt nice in her mouth. She liked the way the vowels swam, curling her tongue. Her feet twist more, and more tarp goes up around her ankles, right up to her knees. She can see the drawer where the spoons live when they aren't being put into mouths or given baths, she can see the handles that's pulled to liberate them, but it keeps moving back a little bit at a time and now it's miles away, and Martha considers that this might be the end of her. The tarp swims and whirlwinds around her. Now it's up to her little girl nipples. Every muscle contraction makes the sound of ocean waves, yes she is wading in the Gulf of Mexico or maybe the Pacific Ocean, and where are her floaties? Martha doesn't know how to swim, and now she panics. Now she struggles even more, and the worst part is she hasn't even tried the cakes. Not a single one of them. It's a travesty. A tragedy. She can see her cake maze out the window and the tarp is only rising its anger. Martha is immobile. Now she cannot move. The tarp becomes thicker, gathering in density, with the greatest intensity and velocity, spinning around her and she can't move. She can't get away. An ocean of plastic bites her mouth. Already it has eaten her button and her armpits, oh no! She wants to stand strong and tall, to resist. She could be *le resistance*, a lighthouse bobbing in the sea, an angry tumultuous sea, and Martha knows nothing about the ocean. She only knows about rivers—and just one river, too. It's not a river like this. This is an ocean, and usually the Rio doesn't even have water in it. It's just a basin that shines under the moon. She wants to resist, so badly. She wants so badly to resist.

But she lets go.

She has to.

She has no other choice.

She can't stand it.

She can't even stand.

And so she pisses herself.

And her bed.

Martha wakes up.

Without spoons or cakes or books or dreams.

Martha wakes up.

Her bed is dry and her eyes are wet.

And Erwin?

He's gone.

~

Ours is a house of silence now.
 Not a single baby cries.
 Because not a single baby lives.

~

When I walk through the house, it is a maze of empty rooms.

MARTHA, CONFINED

This is a list that contains no endings, only beginnings.

This is a list of causes, because everyone already knows its effects.

These are the things that confine you, Martha, the things you chain inside.

~

The spotlight falls on the victim: these are the hot spots of despair. The sun flares, and even the Solarians must shield their eyes from all this woe, these sources of sadness, a weight that only knows how to grow.

1. This is the day you learn that some mamas create out of spite—to hate. This is the day you are born.

2. Like the mobile of animals you never had, the touch you do not know to desire.

3. You coo at your mama's face, and she makes herself ugly back at you. You cry. She leaves.
   You always lose this game.

4. A sketched memory of the light aura of your mama leaving your room, and you not knowing if she will ever return.

5. It is not for you.

6. "Freak," is said, and you know it is said about you.

7. Your mama looks at you and sighs.
   She's too tired to deal with your shit, so she goes away. You don't know what else to do. You cry.

8. "No, no," your grandmother says. "Not freak. Cake. Say it. Cake."
   "Cake," you say. You say, "Cake!"

9. She bakes you a cake.
   Everyone bakes you a cake.
   All day long you sing, "Cake cake cake."

10. Mostly, when you cry, nobody comes.
    If you cry in a house and nobody hears you, is anyone there? Is a house still a house? Are you even crying?

11. The thrill from the cake doesn't last forever. Eventually, the

sugar dissolves and beneath its echo is what makes you an abnormality, a freak, too fat already for anyone's liking, and when you mama says you're a freak, you know what she means. You understand what she's saying.

She says, "Where did you even come from?"

You say, "Cake?"

12. Not a defiance of expectation: a complete rejection.

Your cry softens until you quiet. Your brain is your only friend now, just the dialogue of your limited vocabulary recycled in permutation and repetition—again, again.

There isn't any point, is there?

13. You eat it all.
One fistful at a time.

14. Your grandfather is talking, but he's never talking to you. He hates you. You know this. "You should've never made it."

"She's just a little girl, Daddy. Don't go calling her 'it,' please."

"That thing ain't no little nothing."

You think in your head. Yes, you should have never been made.

15. When your mama isn't being mean to you, her touch is gentle. You belong to her. You really do.

16. "Clap your hands for cake, little freak, clap your hands for cake."

You follow orders very well. Maybe this will make them love you.

17. "She's three times your size when you was her age."

"Well, what am I supposed to do about it?"

18. Must be that you're asking too much.

19. You tell your mama you love her.

She says, "Baby girl, you don't have it in you to love. You don't know how. But that's not your fault, now is it?"

She says, "I know this about you because I'm your mama and I know everything about you. You can't hide nothing from me."

She says, "Remember. I made you."

20. It's Christmas. You don't get a single present. It's OK though because you don't even know you're supposed to get presents today, and you can't miss what you never knew.

You don't know it's Christmas.

It's a day, just like every other day, absolutely nothing notable.

21. Like the time your mama goes, "You destroyed me."

22. The day hums along, a yawn so long and deep it takes two hands to cover it up.

23. Your mama goes, "Completely ruined me."

Surely, she can't be talking about you, her baby girl, her little girl who is just as dumb as a plate.

24. Your mama tells you to make yourself disappear. She says, "Shoo," and you gather all your shoes for her. "Stupid fuck," she says. "Git."

25. You crawl into a chest and hide. The chest is also the coffee table is also the dinner table. Inside, there are quilts and you feel warm. You crush your own body down and down and there is fabric everywhere around you: you are safe here.

26. You laugh at your shoe joke.

Your mama hears you, but she can't hear you because you're hiding.

She hollers, "Pipe it down already."

You are a magician. You are the silent star.

27. Women are hens, just pecking. That's all they know how to do: peck peck peck.

28. When you grow up, will you be happy? Will you go hungry? Who will feed you? If you stop eating, will your mama love you then?

You will stop eating. Today. Right now.

And then your mama will never leave you again.

It's because you're so ugly and fat that your mama can't love you. You know this. Even if everyone didn't say it, you'd know it. But, of course, everyone does say it, and that's why it must be true.

You will never eat again, you promise.

29. She doesn't say goodbye this time. Sometimes, she doesn't say—when she'll come back, if she will, but she will. Maybe. It's a gamble every time.

It's just you and your grandmother now. She is all vitriol, which comes out hot and bright, like the oven set to broil.

30. Your grandfather says, "Shoulda stuck that coat hanger up there myself."

31. Your grandmother prays that the devil will just leave you alone—leave her alone, but she ain't the problem, now is she?

32. When your mama comes back, she says, "No," but you hadn't said anything. You haven't said a single word.

33. The hens are coming over, so your mama tells you to disappear. It's an old trick now, not even fun anymore. You hide in the chest. You feel every glass of lemonade, the slow sweat dripping down onto you. You feel every word, because hens can be very, very mean.

34. You fall down, and no one is there to kiss your boo-boo. No one ever is. It hurts a lot, so you hit it again.

35. Your grandmother says, "You're so gross even your own mama don't want to look at you."

She says, "Why do you think she's always running off?"

You say, "Me."

Your grandmother says, "At least you ain't dumb."

36. And it gets worse every time.

37. Until your grandfather pushes you outside and it's night and it's dark and you can hear the coyote's yowling song swim through the desert breeze.

38. You keep everything inside, like a special secret.

39. When your mama calls you her baby girl, everything curls with delight. Even the tiny mitochondria inside your cells spiral themselves tighter.

40. When your mama cooks for you, the taste makes fireworks going off on your tongue. Yummy.

41. Your grandfather says, "Fucking gross."

She says in response, "Ain't her fault. That one's got the devil inside of her."

42. Your grandfather says, “Get out of my house,” and you do.

    If you listen to him, he won’t push you in the face and kick your side until you roll outside.

    Some lessons only need to be taught one time.

43. Your family is a family of bullies. And this is what you deserve.

44. Some mornings, there is piss all under you. It stinks, and so do you.

45. You used to sleep in the living room, on the loveseat, but today, your grandfather opens up a door in the ceiling and down comes a ladder. He says, “Let’s see if this little piggy can make it up the stairs.”

    Inside, up there, there is a bed. This is your room. Your very own room, all to yourself.

    Your grandfather slams the door. “Now stay up there.”

    How are you supposed to eat dinner?

46. You wait. Something will change. It’s got to.

47. Usually, the hens wait until your mama has left the room, but sometimes, they talk about you even when she’s right there.

    One says, “I think she’ll outgrow it.” She laughs. “Maybe outgrow was the wrong word.”

    They all laugh along.

    Another says, “There isn’t any hope for that one. She’s a lost case.” This time, you can hear your mama’s laugh, too.

48. You don’t want to eat anymore.

    And then you eat again.

    The food in your mouth is spectacular.

    Your tongue is electric. It’s all sparks in there.

No one will love you now, but no one ever did in the first place.

49. It's been days and finally your mama comes home.
She's smaller now than before, you can tell.
She can barely lift you. "Fat pig," she says.
This time, she's not talking about you. She grabs at the skin of her belly. She's talking about herself.

50. Vipers disguised as hens.

51. Your grandmother picks you up, clothes and all, and plops you right into the bathtub. You sink to the bottom. The water is cold.

52. Beaks or fangs, what's the diff?

53. When your grandfather says, "Fat freak," it's so familiar you don't even blink.

54. "If he stays inside you too long," your grandmother says, "even God can't save you." She takes a steel wool pad to your back and arms and the bathwater starts to glow.

55. Your grandfather says, "Git out of my house, you stupid shit."
You open the backdoor yourself and walk outside. You stay there until morning.

56. The hens gab and they gab and you yawn because they are boring. The whole chest trembles with you inside of it.
"An earthquake?"
"Here?"
You can make the earth itself tremble. You are not the devil. You are a god.

57. When you piss your bed, you hide it, just like your mama must be hiding how much she loves you.

58. When your mama is nice to you, sometimes that just makes things worse.

59. Your grandmother says the devil must've made you with his very own hooves.

60. Your mama says, "Let's go feed the ducks."

You scramble for the chance to spend time with your mama. Alone, just the two of you.

You are happy, skipping down the street.

The ducks are happy, quacking about.

The sun is out and playing, too. It is a perfect day.

Your mama says, "Pipe it down already."

You pipe it down. You don't even have a voice anymore.

"Get over here," your mama says. She is sitting on a bench and you pretend you are a duck waddling over to her. She reaches into her purse. She sticks a stale piece of bread in your mouth. "Didn't I tell you to shut up already?"

61. It's late but you aren't sleeping. You're in your bed in the attic and it's starting to smell sour up there.

Your grandfather slams his way into the house.

Your grandmother says something about *pussy* and *money* and *paying* and *whores* and *drunk bastard.* Your grandfather slaps her. You don't see him slap her, but you know the sound of your grandfather's open palm hitting skin so intimately that you could recognize it in a dream, even if you're not dreaming.

62. Your mama is so good at this game. You seek and you seek forever it seems. Where is she?

63. A boy from down the street runs up to you and says, "You look just like a stupid bullfrog."

64. No one has ever called you a good girl.

65. Your grandmother gives you the Bible, says, "Learn to read and maybe this can save you."
    The softness of the paper makes you want to gobble it right up.
    "Probably not though," she says.

66. The devil swims into your dream from deep under the ocean. He looks like a fish. When he opens his mouth, it is filled with red velvet cake.
    He will eat you too.
    You wet your bed. Nothing in your life is right.

67. Your mama brushes your hair every night.
    When she is home—if.

68. One hen says your daddy left because of you. You're the reason he's not there anymore.

69. She bakes you a cake.

70. When your mama brushes your hair, knots come from nowhere. Like one second you've got pretty hair and the next there are a hundred million knots, miniscule like little monsters that get caught in the tines. Your mama starts out patient, but by the time she's pulled the brush through the branches of your hair a few times, each stroke becomes weighted like an anvil.
    Some nights, it only takes an hour. Others, three. Four.

She calls in bonding.

You call it bondage.

You don't know this word yet, but there are words you can feel without naming.

If you could name it, that's what you'd call it: bondage.

71. Instead of dolls, you play with the marbles you stole from the big glass bowl in the doctor's office. You only have a few, but they play with the rocks in the yard, especially late at night if your grandfather puts you out, again.

Everything looks beautiful under the full moon.

72. Your mama tells you that she's moving. And you're coming too! You're moving with your mama and she isn't leaving you behind, not this time. You are so happy you feel sick, like your belly is licorice and twisting. So this is what joy feels like, bliss.

"Where are we going?" you ask.

"Shut your face and go pack," she says. "I leave in thirty minutes, with you or not."

73. A pocket full of marbles; a whole cotton sack of eyes.

74. When your grandmother says, "Slut," it holds the same tone as all the mean things she says to you, about you, but this time, you are innocent. This time, it's not even your fault.

75. Why are you such a bad girl?

76. You have never played house because what would it look like anyway? You don't care to know.

77. A rich man in a rich car drives up to the house and your

mama throws her big suitcase in the back. You run for her, and she shouts, “Too slow, baby girl. You’re just too—”

She blows you a kiss, but the wind is an obstacle course and by the time her kiss reaches you, there is nothing left to catch.

Your palm is dry, but your eyes are not.

78. After church, you come home and the ladder is down. Your room is being invaded! You scamper up the ladder and it’s all OK, everything is OK, except—the sheets are different. They’re purple with stars and gross. You sit down and there’s something under there. It crinkles and there’s an ocean under you, that’s the noise.

Your mama’s head rises from the ground, says, “Mattresses are expensive, baby girl.”

The ocean is going crazy with waves and surf and crashing down.

79. Outside it is snowing. You have never felt so warm before, cuddled tight inside blankets and blankets.

80. “If I wanted to,” your grandfather says, “I could throw your fat ass out right now.”

And then he does it.

But it’s practically a game now: no bigs.

81. There’s a crack and now you’re on the kitchen floor, a big pile of slop.

You’re crying because you fell and it hurts.

You’re crying because now you will never get up to your room again.

Your ladder, splintered everywhere.

And it’s all your fault. Everything is always your fault.

82. She's a prisoner and you are the warden; or is it the other way around?

83. He says, "Better not break this one, piglet," and he pushes a metal ladder into your room. "Can't have you stinking up the place no more. Up."

84. "Tell me, mama, how do I make friends?"
You don't have any friends.
You say, "What if no one likes me?"
"Baby girl," your mama says, "that's just the way it's gonna be for you."
"Help me, mama," you say. You say, "Please?"

85. The new ladder is sturdy. It won't break. But you don't have a door anymore. It's OK. The door never did anything anyway.

86. "Just shut up already."

87. School is rejection, over and over again.

88. "Even my prayers can't help you."

89. You count to zero: that's the exact number of friends you have.

90. A hen says you belong in a circus, that's the kind of freak you are.

91. Your mama lets you go to the store with her. She's going to the mall to buy a new dress. "It has to be pretty, baby girl. Do you want to help me pick it out?"
"Yes, mama, yes!"

She buys you a snow-cone. You drop it in the parking lot and purple ice goes flying everywhere.

92. Hold on. You hold on to what people say. You hold it very tight, it hurts less like that.

93. Daily rejection.
Daily bullying.
Daily crying.

94. Everything you hide.

95. It's lunch time and you walk up to Gloria because she's sitting alone and she's always sitting alone and no one likes her just like no one likes you. She's holding a turkey sandwich to her mouth, opening up her lips, ready to bite. She has black curly hair and a big nose.

You say, "Can I sit with you?"

And Gloria is like, "I'd rather sit alone until infinity ends than sit with you. Ew."

96. Your grandmother calls you a devil, says you have to go to church to get that devil right on out, and maybe then, you'd be decent enough for her to call you her family.

97. Another hen says you're the reason your whole family is poor, because you've eaten everything and, "Be careful," she says, one day you'll probably eat them, too.

98. Pablo is the one who starts it. Pablo with his strong voice that rebounds everywhere and he's got greasy black hair like he never has a bath. He runs around the playground. He is the king, not just today, not just playing around. He is the king every day. You don't like him. He's always mean to you.

It's only the second week of school, but you already understand hierarchy and where you sit in it: the very very bottom. The lowest it goes. Below that, if there's a below that.

You're sitting in the sandbox. You're not looking at Pablo. You're not looking at anyone. You're trying hard not to bother them, the other kids. You are trying your very best to be invisible.

And Pablo is running around like a maniac and he's running toward you. You want to get out of the way. You don't want to be there. He's running fast, right at you. You close your eyes. You wince your face. You almost scream but his voice is faster. It elasticizes around you. "Marge the Barge! Marge the Barge!"

99. Your grandmother points to you with her nose. "You can't see the devil in her?"

The priest looks at you.

You try to look innocent.

He says, "I reckon I just might."

Together, they will purify you. They promise it.

100. You hate the way your mama puts your hair in a bun. None of the other girls wear their hair like that. It wouldn't make them any nicer to you, but maybe.

101. Your mama says your eyes are broken vacuum cleaners. "One look at them and I just get all pissed."

102. These are the things that hold you; the things that hold you back.

103. Your mama spins your hair around her hand. She coils it around the pony tail rubber band. She tucks the loose ends

into somewhere and puts in a thousand bobby pins to keep things in their proper place.

She says, "Now you look almost pretty, baby girl." She winks. "Almost."

104. Your grandmother says, "Pray with me."

You go onto your knees and lower your head and recite the words with her.

105. During recess, the kids sing out, "Marge the Barge," and they pretend to be enormous ships that collide with each other and sink and everybody dies. But you, first.

106. A hen says you scare her. You are the fabric of nightmares.

107. Your mama says you're as dumb as an ironing board. She says, "You don't even know to get out of the way when there's a goddamn hot iron on you." She laughs and it's so beautiful, the sound she can make.

108. Your mama says you're as dumb as a plate, only not as pretty.

109. The pretty girls say you smell like a sewer and you're uglier than a frog. They say you're poorer than a Mexican and just as dirty. They say they would never ever ever want to be friends with you. They pinky swear each other.

You hear all this from the bathroom stall.

They're just young hens, you know this. Hens in training. They are exactly like your mama's friends, just hens.

You want to be a hen, too, but nobody will let you.

110. Your mama says she loves you, calls you her baby girl, that's all that matters, even if you both know she's lying.

111. Peck. Peck, peck.

112. Outside, there's a beautiful leaf swinging in the wind. You are watching it from the inside. You hope the leaf would just fall already. You hope it won't have to endure the humiliation of not belonging. This is how you pray.

113. Janie makes it even worse, "The Barge is docking! Run for your lives!"

And all the other kids, they cheer.

114. Your grandfather makes things fresh and says, "You ain't even my blood. No blood of mine in you, no way."

115. At Confession, the Father lists prayers and you refuse and he says you're doomed to Hell. He says, "If I have any say in it."

116. Another hen says your mama tells her how she regrets you every single day.

117. Mira makes it worse, "Marge the Barge, uglier than she is large."

Who cares anymore? Not you.

118. After all, you agree. You agree with everything.

119. "Like a piece of newspaper under fried chicken, baby girl."

120. She bakes you a cake. You eat it all.

121. At least your marbles aren't mean to you. They're always nice and very round.

122. Antonio kicks sand all over you. He says he's helping you

out. He says, "A face full of sand should make it easier for you to dock." He runs off, fake screaming like he's scared of you or something.

123. It's summer and hot. You have nothing to look forward to, just more of this. You still have no friends. School sucks and now it's vacation. This is it, by the hour, the minute, no faster, no slower, just this.

124. "You'd be better without her."
"I know."

125. Another cake, made just for you.

126. "Mistakes happen."
"She wasn't a mistake."
There's a small leak in the pipe under the sink. It makes you want to pee, and it's so hot under there. You're always hiding somewhere, aren't you?
"Don't lie to yourself, Bernice. You know exactly what she is."
"Yeah," your mama says, breathing out all heavy. "I know."
Your grandmother puts a hand on your mama's shoulder. You can hear how her old skin rubs up against the fake silk. You wish anyone would touch you with the same care and regret.

127. Just the repetitive call of rejection.

128. Your grandfather comes home drunk.
You go outside before he can open his drunk mouth or shove you with his drunk hands. At least it's warm tonight; the stars make picture books for you to read.

129. Ants and mosquitoes and chiggers and fleas and ticks make welts all over your body.

You are so disgusting.

Plus, you itch.

130. Your grandfather opens the backdoor and his outline is blacker than even the black night. He looks at you. He pretends to gag. And then he gags for real and he stumbles at you and he throws up everywhere.

He points at you, says, "You have until morning."

It's so dark still. Dawn isn't here yet, taking her sweet fucking time.

He goes back inside, and by morning, he won't remember a thing. But most of all, you wish you didn't smell like puke.

131. Juan throws a cup of water at the back of your head. You're drenched. The water is cold. He says he wanted to know if a human barge can really float.

He's not clever or funny. It's a stupid joke, but the other kids laugh anyway.

132. While your mama is brushing your hair, you ask her again how to make friends.

"People just like me," she says. "I guess. I don't know, baby girl. How do *you* make friends?"

"I don't," you say.

"Of course not," she says. She finds a thick knot and starts picking at it with her fingers. "Try to not be dumb as a plate. That's a good place to start."

Without resolution, she brushes your hair for another hour.

You don't sleep on a pillow because your head hurts that bad.

133. Your grandmother drops you off in front of the church. She says, "Stay." Like a dog, you stay. You stand there for almost five hours. Sometimes, you have to sit down because your legs get tired real easy.

In the car, she asks, "What'd you learn?"

You think, "Patience."

134. Robert says you're so fat you'd break a crucifix.

135. Another hen says, "It's not too late for adoption."

Another hen says, "Shush. You're so bad."

They squawk.

136. Your mama says, "I ain't disappointed you half as much as you disappointed me." Her hair is all fluffed up and her make-up is perfect. She picks up a lighter and says, "This is how much I've disappointed you, baby girl," and then she points to the oven, "and that's the sadness I feel when I look at you."

She gets up and walks away.

She turns back and says, "That's just a metaphor, though. You're way worse than a stupid oven."

137. Alicia says you look like a used-up parachute that wouldn't even, like, open like it was supposed to. She says, "It's like you're a killer or something."

138. Maria says she wishes you would just die.

Those are the words she used. She actually wishes death upon you.

What did you do?

There is no such as fairness. Justice may as well be a fairy tale.

139. "I really don't even like them, you know?" your mama says as she's brushing your hair. "It's like, I guess everyone needs friends, right? They ain't perfect, but—Jesus, baby doll, look at the size of this one!"

140. Gym is pretty much the worst thing in the whole entire world.

141. Your grandfather hands you a piece of plywood. It isn't a door, but it's something. You say, "Thank you."

He says, "I'm too tired of your fucking stinking up the whole damn house. Needs to stay confined to one place up there, like you piggy."

This is kindness.

142. During recess, Gloria and Janie tie a belt around their little waists.

They wobble around the playground. They charge at a group of kids just standing around, scream, "Marge the Barge! Marge the Barge! I'm gonna crash into you! Wooosh!"

All the kids scatter at this fake version of you.

All the kids scatter at you, too.

143. You are the smartest girl in class. Smarter than all the boys, too. This only makes everyone hate you more, just when you were thinking there was no way things could get worse—but there she goes, up and up. You hold the railing tight.

144. Another hen says she can't believe how *big* you've gotten.

Big means unlovable.

145. Your mama disappears again, and you don't care. Because there will always be a next time.

146. Your mama still isn't back and you have a bad dream and you piss your bed and you can't even remember the dream but it was bad, really bad, and the tarp under you just makes it all worse because it holds the stinky piss in pools.

Before, you used to be able to get back to sleep.

Now, it feels like you're swimming in an ocean, a dirty stinky ocean with lots of jellyfish and sharks and things that want to bite you until you are just meat.

147. "Satan's in here." You point to your chest. Your grandmother slaps you across the face.

148. You put on your raincoat. You put on your backpack. The bell has rung and finally you get to go home. You don't really want to go home, but no one has been mean to you today, so it's been a very good day.

You put your hands into your pockets, and yuck! Something is in there. Something gross, all rough and wiggly, and you don't even know what to do. You really don't.

But you have to know. You need a plan.

All the other kids are watching you, eager for a good laugh.

You have to do something.

You try not to look panicked but you're totally icked out but if anyone saw how you are feeling in your belly, they would laugh and laugh and you'd be the joke, again. You keep your face hard and still.

You wait until everyone else is gone, and then you look inside.

You count out ten lizards, two still alive.

When you get home, you take the lizards out, one by one—by now all ten are dead—and make little graves for each one. You scoop the dirt away with your fingers. You place the lizards in, one by one. You are gentle when you bulldoze the dirt into the holes.

You hate these lizards. It's not like it's their fault, but you hate them anyway.

You hate those bullies for killing the lizards, just for a cheap laugh. You hate death, and then you hate that you had to deal with its aftermath.

You hate, a lot.

Your bullies are evolving, but you are not. Not fast enough.

Outside, a monsoon begins to fall.

149. Your grandmother says she wants to wash you in holy water, except she doesn't like to waste.

150. Your mama says you're moving and then you do and it's wonderful. It's bliss. And not five weeks later, you're back on your ocean mattress. Every night there's a fresh nightmare waiting.

151. During recess, all the girls play jump rope. Or hopscotch. You watch from behind a mulberry tree. You want to play, you really want to play, especially with them, but you know they won't let you so you don't bother to ask. And they wouldn't just say, "No," you know they'd be much meaner than simple rejection. No, those girls are evil, but they sure are pretty while being it.

152. Deflated. You feel deflated: now if only someone could please just deflate you.

153. You and your mama go out driving and drive for a long time. When you open your eyes again, there are big trees everywhere. You pick up a pinecone. "What is this, mama?"

"I shouldn't have taken you with me."

"I'm sorry, mama. I'm sorry."

"For what?"

You think, "For being all wrong." You put the pinecone in your pocket. It sits on your lap all the way home.

154. You sink to the bottom of the pool and nothing happens and you start to freak out and your breath shrinks and your eyes ache and your arms and legs are crazy fools dancing around a disco.

"At least we know she's not a witch," your grandmother says.

"Maybe we should just leave her down there."

155. Tomorrow is your birthday and you ask your mama for a party. She laughs until the carpet shakes and you fall down. You fall down and slide all over the place. Everything is shivering like it's cold, but it's summer and hot hot hot. Your mama can't stop laughing. You will never get a birthday party. You guess that's OK because who would come to your party anyway? You guess, "No one."

156. Your grandmother decides you can't eat at the table anymore.

She puts your plate on the floor, in a corner.

She doesn't tell you to face the wall, but she doesn't need to.

157. All the hens cluck in agreement.

158. Gabe sticks out this leg to make like he's going to trip you. You see him do it, but you can't stop. You can't make yourself stop because you're already going, straight in line and going strong. With purpose. You want to stop yourself or even get out of the way, but you can't. There's just not enough time.

And he pulls his leg back in.

You stumble anyway—over a phantom leg, a ghost leg, it wasn't even there.

Gabe says, "I didn't want to catch a scar from a crash with HSS Martha."

Everyone laughs along, even the teacher sneaks a sly chuckle in there.

159. Your mama says, "Can't you at least try?"

But you are trying. This is the best you can do.

160. "Even Jesus rejects your love, girl," your grandmother says, "and He loves everyone."

161. Tommy says your farts smell better than you do, that's how bad you stink just on your own.

162. Janie says Tommy is wrong.

You hold your breath with hope.

And she's like, "Well, to tell the truth, I've never smelled anything as sick as Martha before, until I smelled her farts that is, and those are like way worse, until I smelled her breath, and that's like double way worse than her farts, until I smell her hooha from like a mile away and I just had to start running."

163. One hen says, "If she weren't so fat, she's got a pretty enough face."

"Pretty enough for what?" They titillate.

164. Rico says you smell like a thousand fish must've died in your mouth.

You cup your hands around your mouth and breathe out hard. It doesn't stink like anything at all, but you stop talking in class, unless the teacher calls out your name.

165. Your mama calls you a dope.

And then she touches your face all nice.

She tucks a few loose hairs behind your ear, says, “But you can’t help that, now can you?”

166. Janie says your hair looks like rotten corn. She asks if it’s like that on its own or if you have to do something special to make it so rotten.

167. Fat cow.

168. A hen says maybe you’re an alien.

169. When you ask your mama to let you cut your hair, she brushes it for twice as long.

170. Your grandmother prays the rosary all day, from before the sun rises until darkness settles and calms.

171. “Gross,” Ariel calls out, because she says you have mudbutt but all over your entire body.

172. Maria pinches her nose and Joanne uses her hand as a fan to circulate the air around her, the air you have contaminated.

173. There’s not a single happy memory in here.

174. Rudy throws dirt at your face, and for no reason, Janie says, “Stop it.” And he does. She says no one should pick on you anymore. She says, “Capisce?”

After school, Rudy says he’s sorry and he gives you a hug and he’s being so nice to you it hurts and walking home every kid runs up to you and kicks you. When you get home, your grandfather kicks your butt real hard, pulls a sign off your back. “Just following instructions,” he says.

175. That time you thought everything was going to be OK—

176. "Oh, baby girl," your mama says, and her voice tells you she knows exactly how you're feeling right now.

177. Humiliation isn't so different from sadness isn't so different from alienation isn't so different from torture. This is torture, your whole life.

178. When Janie doesn't show up to school, everyone says it was your fault—because she was being nice to you that day. "Your evil is like the flu. Keep away from me!"

This is the day they call you Scarlet Martha, because you have the plague.

179. Fez says he doesn't even know why Janie was ever nice to you. He says, "I bet she'd be here today right now if it wasn't for you." He cocks his chin at her.

180. Gloria says you rolled over her and killed her.

181. An idea, one little seed, and look at how it can flower.

182. You don't care about all the mean things the hens say about you anymore, so you don't bother hiding in the chest when they come visit. You don't fit anyway. You're way too fat. Besides, they're just a bunch of stupid hens. Who wants to be like them? You do. You want very much to be like them, but no one lets you in. No one lets you play. But one day, Martha, one day you will be queen of chicken coop, and let's just see what mean things they say about you then.

When you think about punishing them, you feel like a

queen, exactly what you are, studied in the knowledge of justice.

183. Carlos says you're a fat monster.
It's barely even a diss.
You don't run to the bathroom.
You don't start crying.
You don't even look away. You say, "Thank you," like he's just said the nicest thing in the world to you.
His face falls, becomes serious. And he runs. He doesn't yell anything. He doesn't perform any acrobatic jokes about your fat. He just runs away, and fast.

184. When the bell rings, you crumple the paper into a ball and save it in your pocket.
If it looks like trash, no one will open it up. No one will straighten the paper. No one will look at the picture you drew.
If it looks like trash, it will be yours to keep forever.

185. You can't miss what you never knew. You don't even know about it at all.

186. The nights you huddle next to the pecan tree in your yard and start talking to your marbles. They don't say anything nasty back at you because they don't say anything at all.

187. Your grandfather doesn't say a word to you anymore.
There's a good memory!

188. Joanne asks if you live in a trashcan. "Your clothes look like yesterday's garbage."

189. Frankie says it's like you live with skunks or something.

190. Your grandfather says, "Well I ain't feeding her no more."
"Fat chance that'll work."
And they all start laughing, the whole family laughs.

191. Janie is gone for one and a half weeks and when she comes back, she hates you more than ever. You can tell—it's not just the mean things she says, her hate for you ripples out of her in all the directions.

192. Your grandmother says you need to diet.

193. Your gym teacher at school calls you fatty-pants. Like that's a new one.

194. Your mama says you need to eat less.

195. Later, she bakes you a cake, but it's smaller than usual.

196. Coach Gomez makes you do extra jumping jacks and she makes you run for longer than all the other kids.

197. The nurse at school talks to you about nutrition, pulls out the food pyramid and points to each one and talks.

198. Name it, you've heard it: fat, fatso, fatty, fatsy, obese, disgusting, lardface, tub of lard, whale, pig, butterball, Marthaboll, roly-poly, porky, Porky Pig, slob, slobberface, stout, heavy, hefty, bubblerhead, piggy-wiggy, barn, cow, hippo, rhino, elephant, huge, fatass, dumpy, heavyweight, healthy, hog, whopper, fatgirl, fatface, husky, elephantbutt, bear, beast, chunky, fathog, used up grease, heavy, Humpty-Dumpty, poly-woly, portly, pufferfish, rotund, too damn fat, too damn ugly, just plain ugly, the ugliest, etcetera.

You have been hit with sticks and you've had some rocks thrown at you and then—all those words, too. They give you bruises and they make you angry.

199. Is there no such thing as honor? Ethics play harmony to the melody of selfishness.

200. Arlen says you're worse than cancer.

201. You are a stupidhead. Everyone agrees.
202. "Never again," you say. No one is there to respond.

203. Your grandfather calls you a lezzie, nothing new to report.

204. Your grandmother says your entire life is a sin, from the moment you were born you were already sinning.

205. You tell yourself to erase all these bad times. Erase them completely.

206. Life makes its lessons to you in perforations so severe you think you might leak out until nothing is left in you, nothing in you left, you are left with nothing.

   Hours pass this way, days. Minutes. No matter the interval of time, it all feels exactly the same: intolerable.

207. Janie balks at you, and the other kids are copycats.

208. You're just a stupid fat girl who makes good grades. So maybe you're not really that stupid but that doesn't you any less fat.

209. Anna says you're a whale, and you are.

210. Your mama stops giving you lunch money.

She's talking about all the food you eat. She's talking about the money. She says, "Every little bit helps."

211. No one talks to you.

212. In school, everybody likes to talk about you.

213. There goes your mama again, right on out the door.

214. Knowledge isn't important sometimes. Facts don't mean shit to kids. Kids are all intuition and spite.

215. Carlos throws an armful of dirt in your hair.

216. Then, Juan, Carlos's twin brother, throws a cup of curdled chocolate pudding on top of the dirt. He says, "Wouldn't waste the fresh stuff on you, freak. Dream on."

217. The moon is big and flammable, that's how electric orange it is.

 "Stupid as a plate," you say. You point your finger at it in accusation.

218. Kendra traps three snakes inside your desk. They aren't poisonous or anything, but you don't know the difference.

219. Your mama takes you away and promises to never make you go back to your grandparents' house. "All that crazy devil talk," she says. She smokes on a cigarette and it smells like pine needles and coal. Your mama drives with you for hours and then you two get out of the car and walk into a diner and you get pancakes and a big slice of chocolate cake, too. Afterwards, your mama gives you the keys and tells you to go to the car and get into it and start the engine. Afterwards,

your mama walks real fast out the restaurant and you two drive away. You knew exactly what was going on, and you let it happen anyway.

This also means you are out of money and so your adventure is about to be over. You're about to end up right back where you started: in a pissy bed without a door.

220. Amelia calls you a fat rat. Isn't her rhyming clever?

221. Maria runs around the playground with a dart. She passes it from person to person. She is offering two whole quarters to the first person who can pin the dart to the Mart, that's you, Mart being a truncation of Martha. It's not very clever, but then again, Maria's pretty stupid.

222. A homeless man sees you and asks you for mercy.

You say, "Go get a job."

He says, "I tried, I really tried, but who's going to give a man like me a chance? Come on girl, show me a little love."

"Altruism," you say, "is for fools and degenerates." You go home.

223. Lorraine says you want to be an ugly slut, except no boy would ever kiss you.

224. Jose says, "She has syphilis."

225. Arlen says you can't have syphilis because who would be dumb enough to touch you? "You might get pregnant if you touch her," he says, "and then you'd have a retarded baby!"

226. Later, oh, what Arlen will do for you, Martha: wait for it: he's going to ruin you.

227. Penny says your mom is a stupid bitch.
 You slap her face for talking bad about your mama.
 She goes, "You're a stupid bitch too. And fat."

228. Christian says it's a shame you were born.

229. You always hide during recess. Don't you want to go out to play?

230. You can't believe people still call you "Marge the Barge." You can't believe they haven't come up with something smarter than that yet. It's such an old anthem, everybody knows the words.

231. Sometimes, you hope a hero will come save you. He doesn't have to be handsome or a prince. He can be just anyone. He doesn't even have to be a boy. It could be anybody. You're desperate.

232. Your mama says, "Baby girl, you got nothing. I gave you everything and got nothing to show back at me. So let your poor mama have your hair. Give me this one thing to be proud of you for."

233. Brian says you look like a lump of powdered mashed potatoes.
 It's all in the details.

234. Your mama says you're not allowed to eat cake anymore. Not until you start looking less like an animal. She says, "You look like a goddamn animal."

235. In the bathroom, a teacher says, "It's not like I don't feel bad for her, you know. Those kids are really mean to her."

The other says, "You don't think she deserves it?"

They powder their noses and freshen their lips and you imagine their reflections in the mirror are beautiful.

236. Your mama calls you a beast, but so does everyone in your family.

237. It doesn't matter where you are. Mean words find you. Every mouth is a potential threat.

238. You uncrumple a note thrown at your head. You make it into a tight ball in your fist. You hold it there until the bell rings and everyone else leaves.

239. Coach Garza tells you to do ten sit-ups. Everybody has to do it. No exceptions. "It's a state thing," she says. These are the worst. You can't do even one on your best day and now the whole class is staring.

You plop down to the mat and roll over onto your back. You tighten every bit of your belly, take a deep smacking breath in, and let out all the air and pull you head as hard as you can up to your knees.

But you are immutable.

You try again. The cruelest inhale, the crudest exhale, and then bad-a-bing like magic you're up at your knees. The class erupts. They're clapping, and it's for you! No one is laughing. It's a miracle. You fall back down. You manage three whole sit-ups, which means you fail the assignment like a lot, still it feels like winning.

240. Paul drops to the mat and does ten sit-ups like they're easy. Anyone can do it.

241. The hens are coming over again, your mama says. It's been a

while so you think maybe it'd be fun to listen in for a while. You climb into the chest. It's tight in there. You shut the door, and the wood catches on your fingers. The doorbell rings and all you hear is artificial flavors, not a single splinter of honesty, your mama and her friends, they're fake fakers, all compliments and ragtime stories.

Is this your future, too? Is this what it means to be a woman? This is what it means to be an adult.

You close your eyes and pay extra careful attention.

242. One hen says, "There's no such thing as too skinny."

Another says, "Bernice, I don't know how you do it, girl. You are just so skinny and perfect. The problem is—"

And your mama stops her before she can finish. Your mama is about to defend you. You're a fool to believe this. Your mama goes, "Yeah, girl's just a freak."

243. "God didn't make everything because there's no way He made you."

244. You lay down flat on your bed.

From nowhere, there's something pressing down on your chest.

Your heart is bulging around.

Your breath can't catch itself.

Your body is soapy sweat and stinky.

You panic. You don't know what's happening. You're about to call for help but you can't open your mouth at all. Nothing works. Maybe you have cancer, you don't know. Someone needs to come help you.

You're frozen, totally stuck, dumb as a plate and just so damn ugly and fat.

245. Instead of feeling scared anymore, you just hate—all of it.

246. Over breakfast, your grandfather calls you a hog. He says, "Shove an apple in her mouth and a spit up her ass and there ain't one lick of difference between them two."

247. Over breakfast, your grandmother won't look at your face. But at least you can sit at the table again. For now.

248. Janie walks into class and you flush immediately. She's wearing the prettiest cotton candy and tangerine dress, all air and sugar and fluff. She is more than a goddess, looking like that, more impressive than Athena and the rest of them, too. She doesn't look your way, not even once; she is all you can see.

In Math class, Missus Rodriguez asks Janie a question in front of the class, and even though she gets the answer wrong, the whole class claps because at least she tried. Everybody loves Janie, especially you. You scowl at the back of her head.

249. She whispers, loud enough so everyone can hear it. "Lesbo."

250. Your mama comes home and who cares how long it's been, not you. Her skin dazzles with sunlight and her hair is as white as a hot flame. Then she sees you and everything darkens. She walks into another room, and you can hear her sighs. Maybe she's crying, too, but you can't hear that good.

251. Janie was only nice to you for a day. You hate her for that. Better to have never been nice to you, that would've been better. Janie made you think someone could be your friend, and not just anyone but the best girl in the entire school, and now, she hates you even harder than everyone else. You hate her for that. You hate her for everything. You just hate.

252. She says you're so ugly even dogs don't want to pee on you. She says you make them barf as soon as they see you. She says you make her want to barf right now, and she makes like she's about to hurl a big one.

253. Your grandmother tells you she's going to stop praying for you.

You say, "It's OK. I'm hopeless."

"I just gotta lure the devil out of you, girl. You'll get all better, just and see. Pray with me, girl. Now it's time to pray again."

The kitchen clock just keeps on marking time away. Its hands tick and turn.

"But I don't want to," you say.

She hits the back of your legs until you are on your knees, with her, in prayer.

254. You are at the store with your mama.

Outside, the heat scorches at your skin, kissing you, welting you.

Inside, there's a nice cool that slurps your sweat. It makes your skin all itchy.

Your mama goes to the baking section, so you head straight for the bakery. She's not watching you. It's not a problem.

In front of the bakery case, there's another little girl. She's not white, she's not like you. She's not Mexican either. She's darker than you, than them, and you think she has beautiful skin: it's dark like how you can't see because you're sleeping and your eyes are closed and no lights are on, and all that's put right there, right on her body. It's like she's scary, because all those things are scary and stunning at the same time: you are stunned, too.

You walk up to her. You look at the tres leches cakes and flans.

You say, "Which one of these do you think looks most delicious?"

"You shouldn't talk to me none," she says. She makes a gesture with her eyes, like she's bad news or something.

"Why?" you ask.

The baker is wearing a white apron and his hands have flour on them.

"But I really wanna talk to you," you say. "I think we can be friends."

She tells you she has enough friends.

She tells you to leave her alone, but she isn't mean about it.

She walks away, but then turns around. She says, "I like the strawberry donuts. They're really good here."

You order a piece of double chocolate cake and eat it in the store so your mama doesn't have to buy it.

255. Your grandmother never gives up, she just dies, eventually—later, not too much later, but later enough to cause you to suffer more now. No, you'll need to endure more devil talk for ages and ages. You anguish every single time.

256. He's like, "She's so fat that one more pound and she could drop a freight elevator."

And she's like, "You really think so?"

And he's like, "Just one more pound should do it, yeah."

It's no bigs, they're just talking like anybody else would.

257. No one has called you beautiful.

258. Or even pretty. Or nice.

259. Your grandfather says, "If I didn't care at all, I wouldn't bother kicking your fat ass out."

He says, "That's when you really got to start worrying."

He says, "Now git the fuck away from me before the devil starts coming into me."

260. If anyone was ever nice to you, you know they wouldn't mean it. Employing irony, or something.

261. Janie doesn't say anything to you, just starts screaming when she sees you at recess, makes it out like you could kill her if she looks at your face for even one more second.

262. Rejection partitions itself into donuts and slices of cake. Some contain more rejection than others, each melancholic bite.
    So you eat them all.
    You swallow before you take another bite.

263. They throw sticks and rock and sand and dirt at your back.
    You're not kidding yourself: they'd throw it at your front too, but you're too busy running away.

264. "Crazy and large!"

265. You could kill them all, the whole swarm of them.

266. "Run for your lives!"

267. "Ain't her fault."
    Whose is it then?

268. You pray with her.

269. When it isn't a school day, you're praying all day long. Ten million rosaries, going by like a merry go round.

270. Your grandfather goes, "Scram."

271. She heaves and she hoes and blood freckles up to your scalp where hair used to be.

272. Summer is even worse than the very worst.

273. Can you imagine? Until you live it.

274. Missus Rodriguez hands back the math quizzes and of course you didn't get a single question wrong. You feel happy today because Janie is sitting behind you and even though she pretends you're not there, at least she's close.

275. It's hot outside. You hate the hot.

It's dry outside. You hate that, too.

276. You think you must hate the big hens more the little hens, but one day they'll grow more and so you'll have to hate them more then. "That'll be easy," you think. It won't be hard at all.

277. Missus Rodriguez hands back the math quizzes and of course you didn't get a single question wrong.

Behind you, something like a fly goes by your neck, barely touches it. You pull your head back to be closer.

A fly could be a friend. Why not?

You smile.

You feel warm.

And then—lightness.

And then—Janie's running around the room all crazy. There's something yellow and stringy in her hand.

She looks radiant.

She looks like Miss America, right after they put the crown on her.

Like she's about to cry, she's too happy.

You don't know how to feel: gratitude or despair.

278. It hurts, more or less the same as always.

279. "Is it always gonna be like this?" you ask.

She says, "Yes."

280. At least it's not in front of your face.

You still hear it, sure, but they don't see you because you're in hiding.

281. You wish you were a bear and could hibernate and no one would bother you.

282. You'd kill anyone for trying.

283. You growl. Is everyone scared yet?

284. You get two answers wrong on the math quiz today. It'll be five tomorrow. It doesn't matter. No one cares about math. You hate it.

285. "It's what you always wanted, ain't it, baby girl? Couldn't even give your mama one little thing."

She throws all the brushes in the trashcan, even your toothbrush.

You'll have bad breath, just like they always said.

286. A curse in promises.

287. You've never hooked your pinky together with anyone else's in your life.

Skin in notches of forever. Oh, fuck them all.

288. Your hair is gone and you hate hair.

Your hair is gone but your neck is still sticky. You hate sticky things. On you, especially.

Janie cut it off and you hate Janie.

Missus Rodriguez gave you an A on your quiz. You hate Missus Rodriguez.

Missus Rodriguez gave you a C on your quiz. You hate Missus Rodriguez.

The sun is high over the clouds during recess. You hate the sun even more than you hate the clouds, every different kind. You hate recess. You hate it a lot.

You hate the sidewalk and the grass, the dirt underneath it and the air above it. You hate every kid in your class, you hate every adult. You hate babies for being born and old people for dying. You hate every baby that will be born in the future and you just hate old people for being old. You hate wearing shoes and you hate being barefoot. You hate socks, too. You hate cake because you can never get enough of it. You hate being a pig. You hate money and you hate being poor, you hate Truth or Dare, a game you've never even played but you know about it from TV and from books. You hate games. You hate TV. You hate books. You hate Janie, you hate her so much. You hate her parents for making her and letting her grow all pretty. You hate your mama and your grandmother and your grandfather, he's the biggest asshole in the world. You hate him maybe as much as you hate your daddy, but you don't know who he is, and you hate that more but maybe you'd hate it less, no one gave you the choice. You hate all men because any of them could be your daddy. You hate your fat face and the way you chew food.

You hate the trees and the flowers and the river and park benches and glass and water and ducks and watermelon and drinking fountains and all the people who use them who don't look like you, who aren't fat like you and white like you and girls like you and named Martha, like you. You hate them because you're icky and they know it. They look at you like you're the worst. You're the problem. You hate them all because they know it, too. You hate hierarchy and you hate being white trash. You hate the president for ruling and you hate princesses that get to marry princes. You hate the vice president, too, anyone who makes rules, you hate. You hate teachers and you hate yourself for trying. You hate that you have to breathe air in order to live. You hate living. You hate life. You wish everything would just go and die already, especially you. Dead dead dead, you hate Janie. You hate her pretty nails and her swift tongue. You hate food stamps and you hate the poor. They're just lazy. They live off the system and you hate the system. You hate happy books for being happy. You hate them when they're sad and scary. You hate being scared. You hate all the kids and adults for making you scared. You hate hens most of all, but maybe you hate some other things more. It's possible that you hate possibility. You hate sweat and socks, you hate wearing socks. You hate clothes that don't fit. You hate being fat. You hate that all the kids tease you, you hate kids and teasing and adults. You hate old people. You hate everything and everyone but especially Janie. You hate Janie most. You think maybe you should hate your mama more, just for making you at all. But who cares about fairness or anything at all? You hate justice and you hate it being gone. You hate Janie, you hate Janie some more. There's a price to be paid when you mess with Martha Jelinski: you've never felt this way before. This must be the desire for justice, you hate justice. You hate judges and juries and lawyers and the law. You hate hate hate Janie.

You want her to suffer. You want her to say she's sorry. You want her to be your friend, you'd forgive her, oh yes you would. You hate forgiveness and so you make a plan, a perfect plan and it will take planning and timing, and Jesus you hate time. You can wait though, Jesus fucking Christ you can wait. You can have patience just this once. You hate once and once upon a time and you hate Janie and flossing and tartar sauce and yellow mustard and hot dogs and math quizzes and homework and playing and all the no ones who don't play with you and your grandfather's stinky whiskey breath and your grandmother's cunt and your mama's touch. You hate it every time she touches you. Ever. You hate Janie, yes you do. You hate food and plates and how your mama says you're as dumb as one because that's just stupid and you hate it when your mama's stupid and you hate all her stupid friends. You hate her boyfriends for making her cry. You hate it when you cry. You hate yourself because you make your mama cry but that makes you happy too. You hate that she says you've ruined her life and you have but she's ruined yours just the same and you hate her for that. You hate mirrors for telling the truth and you hate mirrors on the wall. You hate fairness and you hate mirrors that tell you lies. You hate stories and happy endings and you hate Disney and cartoons because they're so pretty. You hate yourself. You hate yourself most of all. You hate drawing, you hate pictures that move, you hate the ones that stay still forever. You hate television and the radio and sound, you hate sound. You hate four-leaf clovers for being hard to find. You hate three-leaf clovers for being common. You hate. You hate.

You hate.

Without respite, you hate.

289. You bellow out, "I hate you." There's no one there to receive it.

290. She calls you a retard and maybe she's the retarded one, but you don't say anything. You just swallow it whole. She has a whole rack of friends to protect her from the Barge that's docking. You have only you, just you—as always.

291. He says you're so fat you already have titties but they're not girl titties. "Fat titties," he says.

He says your fat titties are so gross even a pedophile wouldn't touch them.

He says you're so fat that God probably hates you.

Maybe your grandmother was right this whole time. Maybe everyone has been right about you all along.

292. She says you're so gross even the flu doesn't want to infect you.

You can't remember the last time you were sick.

293. You hate being sick.

294. Arlen says, "You're so gross even a leech wouldn't drink your blood."

295. Your mama calls you an egghead because you're always reading books.

You like to read books because they aren't like your life. Your life, you recognize, is miserable. Sometimes, you play pretend that your life isn't your life at all but one that isn't bad. It might even be a book—and then you laugh.

No one would ever ever ever read a book about a fat girl with no friends.

You think maybe this is a turning point.

You will go on a diet, on two thousand diets, and then you'll be prettier than Janie.

And then a rich handsome man will marry you.
And then anyone in the world will marry you.
As if.

296. She says, “She’s even bigger than a barge now. Just look at her.”
Janie says, “It looks like she ate the whole ocean.”
She says, “Like it was easy or something.”

297. He says, “There’s a devil inside you, girl.” He dips his whole hand in holy water and sprinkles in on your head.
Positive reinforcement: you hate it.

298. She says barges are flat boats but you’re just fat, whatever that means.
The other kids laugh at you.
They always do.

299. Janie’s going to pay. You promise yourself that.
You hook the pinky on your left hand into the one on your right hand.
It’s a promise, a way to make a pact for real.

300. You watch the moon at dawn. This is the coldest time of day. It feels like home.

301. You are making your own lunch these days. Your grandmother hasn’t bought new sandwich meat. The cheese has mold on it. You take out two pieces of bread, pour on some mayonnaise, slap the two pieces together: yum.

302. Missus Gonzales says, “Martha, come on up.”
You push at your desk for leverage. It takes you two tries.

She says something about *trying*. She says something about *be more like Martha*.

Crystal raises her hand and stands up tall and says, "I would never want to be like Martha, even if she *is* smart, which she's not. No one so ugly could ever be smart."

Missus Gonzales isn't smart, so she says, "And why not?"

You want to say something. You want this to stop. This is worse than humiliating. You want to beg this time. Please, no.

303. You are the punchline to every single joke because that's just the way it is. Can't be any different. It's just the way it is.

304. Your grandmother says, "You put cancer inside me."

You didn't put cancer inside of her.

She does not have cancer.

But sometimes you wish she would. If you had the devil in you for real, she'd have cancer.

305. She bakes you a cake. Your mama bakes you two. You eat them all.

306. Your grandmother says, "You may not have put any cancer in me, but you were a cancer in your mama and now you're a cancer inside my whole damn house."

You wish your grandmother would just die already, your grandfather, too. You hope it hurts. You hope whatever kills them will make them suffer.

You wish they would die and then you would die and everyone would just be dead.

307. The only thing you can think about is how to hurt Janie. She, above all others, deserves your punishment.

308. Your mama buys you a cake from the store. It doesn't say "Happy Birthday" and there are no candles.

The store uses cheap frosting.

Doesn't matter. Tastes pretty much the same.

309. There are a billion stars out tonight. You think that with all those stars and all the people in the world, surely, you should not feel so alone.

You look for the moon. You twist your head all around. It must be hiding. It must be terribly lonely up there for a moon, surrounded by stars and no other moons to be its friend. "I get you, moon," you say, but the moon isn't close enough to hear.

310. Arlen says, "If you ever touch me again, like ever, even if my skull's cracked open and my brains are rolling out all over the place, do not, I repeat, not, under any circumstances, touch me again. I'd rather die than have you touch me again."

Arlen is so fucking stupid. You hate him, but only as much as you hate everybody else.

311. Your hair is all gone but your mama won't let up her primping. You hair is all gone but your head is still filled with goat's heads and knots: sailor knots, barrel knots, overhand knots, honda knots, Flemish knots, European death knots, fisherman knots, even double fisherman knots. Complex knots. Knots the size of your fist. Knots the size of your thumping heart.

Your mama says, "What the fuck is wrong with you, baby girl?"

You could list out two million reasons right now, easy, but that would just bore her. But maybe then she'll leave you alone. Yes, you would rather her never listen at all than start listening and stop, so you say nothing. You choose to eat your own banality alone, please and thank you. She pulls, fiercely.

312. What you feel is destitution. What you feel is anger. What you feel is betrayal. What you feel is a crude desire for wrath and vengeance against every single bully who's ever said one mean thing to you. What you want is to have their legs cut off at the thigh. What you want is for them to fall to their knees in forgiveness but they ain't got knees left. What you feel is deep and full and savory.

     You name this desire. You call it revenge.

313. Your grandfather has thrown you out again. You look up and think about how most of the stars out there are already dead. It just takes so long for them to get to your eyes that they could be dead already—like dead, dead—and you wouldn't even know because all you can see is how they still twinkle. There must be something profound in there, but you don't know what. You don't know anything, except—dead or not, you hate the stars, all of them.

314. Revenge is just another form of justice.

315. She says you're a fat bitch, and honesty stings.

316. Janie, you really want to hurt her.

317. Planning, planning: plotting.

     It just takes so much of your time.

318. Your grandfather smashes your Science Fair project, and he's not even drunk.

319. She walks up from behind and says something mean. Lisa's stupid though and so are her insults. You don't bother listening to them. No one really cares about her or what she has to say. She's poor and dumb and she's not even pretty. But she doesn't let up. Keeps talking and talking her lame burns on you, like she can't even tell how vapid they are.

Janie comes up. She says, "Just shut up already Lisa. No one cares about you."

You don't understand. How can Janie be nice to you all of a sudden?

But Janie wasn't being nice. She was giving you her pity. "It's not your fault," she says. She says, "Sometimes, I feel so bad for you." You don't want her pity. You wish you could shove that pity right back in her pretty face. She says, "Because you're really as gross as everyone says. But what can you do?" You want to make Janie as ugly as you are.

320. "Red Rover, Red Rover, please don't let Martha come over!"

As if you're all still five or something.

But, that doesn't mean it doesn't slice, but your meat is too bruised for the eating.

321. You hate Wednesdays because it's Mexican food day in the cafeteria. They don't even give you dessert, just a piece of cornbread that's stale.

322. Your skin is raw from all your grandfather's beatings. Your mama draws you a bath, undresses you, says nothing.

323. Your grandmother is back on her devil talk, and it's getting old, all of it: your grandmother being an asshole, your grandfather being an asshole, your mama being an asshole. You are a family of asses.

You say, "What makes you so sure there's a devil in me? What have I done?"

And she says, "It ain't what you doing now, stupid. It's what you're gonna do later, in the future. You're gonna be worse than a monster. It's so bad I can't even think up what you're gonna be. I'm trying to clean all that evil right on out of you. You should be grateful is what you should be."

So you let them tie you to the bed. You let all the Catholic voodoo into your body in hopes of releasing a beast. Your grandmother isn't right about you, but it's like insurance, you know? Just in case.

324. They all agree that your mama is totally trashy.

325. There's a man walking down the street and he looks like you. He looks so much like you that you think he's your daddy. You run up to him, but you're so fat he's gone when you get there.

326. When you and your mama walk into a store, the saleslady goes from little birdie to a storm cloud ready for rain.

327. Maybe your grandmother's right and there's something bad inside you. Why else would no one like you? Why else would you want to hurt Janie and everyone else too? Why else would you have sketches and blueprints and a careful timeline for revenge? Why would you even want revenge?

    Yes, you think, your grandmother must be right about you.

    So you keep hard at work, planning, meticulous planning.

328. You throw up on your desk, and Johnny's like, "Like that's gonna help your fat ass, fat ass."

    He's funny and you have a fever. Doesn't matter.

329. When it's just you and your mama, sometimes she isn't mean, but mostly, you're only a good girl when you shut the fuck up.

"It's better," she says, "when you ain't here at all."

But that kind of defeats the whole point of it.

330. You're so fat you can't even disappear.

331. Ick, and you stink up a whole room now.

332. You see Janie's mama on the street. You know it's her because everyone in town knows who Missus McDonagall is. She looks just like a movie star.

333. He says, "You look like what a caveman musta looked like, before he turned into a human." He says that's what's wrong with you, you belong like a hundred million years ago or whatever, like, before evolution happened.

You want to shove his nose in and break it.

You want to hurt him. What he said wasn't even that bad, but there's this anger inside you now. It's all over your body, and it feels electric.

You say, "You better run, Juan."

You shout this at his face, or, maybe you don't say anything at all.

334. Your grandmother says, "You can never be forgiven."

335. A cake is baked and so you eat it.

336. Your mama says, "Oh, she'll probably grow out it. Just look at me."

You are hidden, but you don't need to see her to know how pretty your mama looks right now. Everything about your mama is perfect: her hair, her face, her delicate nose, her barely bronzed skin, legs like no one's seen before or since, and titties that can barely fit in a big man's hand.

And look at you.

You are grateful to be stuck in a stupid, cramped chest. Only a few streams of light come in, so you can't see yourself, even if you tried, even if you wanted to, which you don't. Why would you?

337. It's getting worse, your anger.

Before, it wasn't anger.

Before, it was sadness. Lingering, hovering, a constant. It sat on your shoulders like a painful companion. For years, you wanted friends—or, just one single friend. You didn't know that sadness could be your friend. It stays with you, always.

And then it wasn't sadness anymore. It grew up. It became something new. It became anger.

Now, you walk around and it always finds you. You don't know where it begins or how to control it. It appears, a solar flare all around your body, and you want to yell, you want to scream, you want to beat your fists against anything. You want release.

You yell.

You scream.

You beat your fists against anything.

But it doesn't help.

Every night you dream of revenge. This is how you will get the devil out of your body. This is how you will become thin and pretty. This is how you will become normal.

338. You wait. You are waiting.

For what?

339. You walk into Social Studies, not bothering anyone at all. Your head is down and someone says, "Look up, loser."

You look up and on the chalkboard, there's a note and it's to you, "Marge the Barge belongs in HELL."

It is an anonymous act of terrorism, which the teacher erases without even a care.

340. "This isn't a good time."

She's crying, your mama. "Mama," you say and run to her side.

"Just get away from me." She pushes you down and you stay there until it's time to get up and go away.

341. Every night you write in your journal your super secret plans to ruin Janie. There are drawings and charts, maps and detailed notes.

You cry and ink runs all over the place.

342. Your grandmother says, "Enough. Go somewhere else already."

You are driving in the car. She stops it. You get out. You have no idea where you're going. You just start walking.

343. Will this ever end?
It must, right?

344. Feelings go smashing around inside you.

345. You wave at a girl on her bicycle and she turns around and says, "You're such an ape." She snaps her head back to the road and pedals as fast as she can.

346. You want Janie, hungry.

347. So hungry today. It can't wait.

348. Simple chocolate is your favorite. No need for anything too fancy.

349. Watching Janie feeds you as much as food.

350. In Science, Mister Barnett is going on about the solar system. He asks what planet is most like you, the one you find affinity with. All of the girls say Mercury, because it's hot and small. A bunch of boys say Earth, because they lack imagination. One or two say Mars, because it's big and red and their favorite drink is Big Red.

  Mister Barnett calls on you.

  You stand up. "I would either be Pluto, because it doesn't fit in, or," you say, "or maybe Jupiter, because it's as large as a barge."

  You have just converted cruelty into power.

  How does it feel?

  It feels like you are Jupiter today.

351. She says your belly must be filled with a whole landfill.

352. She says you should be as extinct as a wooly mammoth.

353. Janie says no boy will ever love you because you're ugly and you're fat and you have a terrible personality. Janie says you will grow up and become an old cat lady or a witch. That's the *best* you can hope for. That's what she says.

354. Josh walks right up to you in Reading.

  You're reading a book, but you were only pretending to read. You weren't really reading at all. You were just watching the other kids in case anyone went trying to start something.

He leans his body onto your desk.

He says he's sorry for being mean to you.

He says he'd like to be your friend now, if that's OK with you.

You think this is a lie, but he smiles at you all nice.

His hair is a whole field of wild peppermint.

You think he's a liar and he's probably laughing at you on the inside. You don't care though. You'll take it, just this one minute of someone being nice to you.

You smile back. You are almost about to cry.

"Psych!"

355. Later, she adds, "Your brain must be a landfill too. That's why your face is so ugly."

356. They use rope to tie your hands and feet together.

The priest talks in Latin. He is screaming and then you are screaming and then neither of you is making any sound at all.

357. Afterwards, your grandmother unbinds you. She helps you stand up. She holds you real sweet. She has never held you like this. You hate her for being an easy con, a tepid fool.

She says, "Was that terrible?"

She puts her wrinkled old hand on your head and strokes it.

"I'm so sorry," she says.

She says, "I love you."

Her words make loops around inside your belly. They churn and undigest. They unfetter something of a devil inside you.

You nuzzle her face deeper into her chest, pure.

358. "Out."

359. Your mama is saying something but you can't hear her because you don't want to anymore.

360. The possibility that the devil *does* live inside you. You're not so scared.

361. It hurts, always.

362. This is what getting caught looks like. This is what being a failure looks like. But you got Janie, yes you did, you got her good. But now you're in jail and how did you get caught? You can't even remember. Maybe your mama was right and you are just dumb as a plate.

Except that getting caught means everyone knows.

Except that getting caught means recognition.

It means that everyone will understand what justice looks like.

It means you are confined, but just for today. For right now.

You, Martha, are confined.

And yet—you feel free, for once, for the first time, relieved and free.

Everything smells like rancid piss. Ah, yes.

363. "Whatever."

364. Etcetera.

365. Because it just keeps on going. It never stops. You think it will, but it won't.

Forever and ever, just like the galaxy.

365.25. People destroy your faith in people. It's their own faults.

MARTHA, IN LOVE

This is what I know: I know what Martha feels. I always understand her emotions, past and present, I see them, but I cannot know her body. I don't know what it felt like, the body that gave us life and then killed us.

But—I know what forced her to do it.

Kenny thinks it was all his fault, and it was.

Martha killed us out of revenge.

Kenny should've never said all those things to her. He should've never fought with her or against her. He should not have hurt her feelings. He should not have given fodder for her thoughts to bloom into murder.

Martha felt like she had no power.

She killed us because she was powerless. This was her only path to power, and it didn't even work. Watching her now, she looks weaker than ever. More pathetic.

She killed us to keep Kenny. She was scared he'd run away and leave her all alone. She thought he didn't love her. It doesn't matter now if he did or not. I guess it never did.

Whereas she just loved him so damn much.

MURDER NO. 1

Affect: "I'm so sorry," says Kenny. "I didn't mean any of it."

Martha feels his apology.

None of it is real, though, or, all of it is.

Kenny says, "I love you."

This is all Martha has ever wanted. Love, his love, in the tendrils of submission. She can see his love weaving through the cells of her body, extending up to the stars.

Martha knows how fickle love can be. Kenny has left her once, and he's bound to do it many more times. There is a map of their projected future projected onto the daisy wallpaper in the kitchen. She is washing dishes.

"I know, baby, I know."

~

Effect: Sudden Infant Death Syndrome.

~

Effect: Little Jimmy is dead.

~

Effect: 250 pounds of flesh on top of flesh.

~

Effect: Sadness washes. It cleanses and purifies. Sadness is good enough.

~

Effect: Kenny does not leave. He does not argue. He is quiet and forlorn. He is guilty. Everything is his fault. Little Jimmy wasn't even his blood, but that doesn't relieve him any. There is no assuaging of a shame so broad.

~

Affect: The scale of bodies, their scale.

MURDER NO. 2

Affect: "It ain't like I don't know what you're doing."

"What? What am I doing then?"

"You think I'm dumb or what?"

Their anger belts through the house. Suzie Ann starts up her wailing, so I run to her room to quiet her before things get real bad. I give her a bottle, and the volume rises all around me.

I hear the walls break glass. Objects in motion halt when forced to.

And there is silence.

"This isn't working."

"Yeah, so what? You gonna go running off again?"

"Yeah, I think this might be a good—"

"A good what? What, Kenny, goddamn it, just say it."

"For me to go."

"That's what I thought. Kenny's always good at going. Goes all damn day and goes all fucking night too, ain't you?"

"No, Martha, really—"

"Good," she says. "Go then. You ain't nothing to me."

"It's just—this isn't working. I tried and can't you see it's not working?"

Suzie Ann is sleeping now.

"What?"

"All of it."

"So what you trying to say?"

"Just, it's not working. I thought I could, Martha, I really—"

Something hard hits the wall, wood against cheap wood. It's the door. The engine rumbles.

~

Effect: Sudden Infant Death Syndrome.

~

Effect: Suzie Ann was just three months old.

~

Effect: 250 pounds of flesh on top of flesh.

~

Effect: Sadness washes. It cleans and purifies. But sadness is rarely enough.

~

Affect: After the funeral, Kenny holds Martha's hand. Tears go out for a stroll; they cross faces and never return.

~

Effect: Kenny will not leave again, he swears it. Suzie Ann was his prize, his little bunny rabbit. He may as well have killed her himself, that's how bad he feels. Inside his head is his punishment, what remains.

Kenny has learned his lesson. This time. Until he forgets, and he will. It's inevitable. Memories lose vibrancy, even trauma bleaches over time.

MURDER NO. 3

Affect: "Just where do you think you're going?" asks Martha.

"Office. There's a little thing to welcome a new doctor. I told you this, babe."

"Little thing, huh? And I take it I ain't invited."

"It's not that. It's just, it's a work thing. No one's bringing—"

"I know what this is about."

"Martha, please."

"You're embarrassed of me."

"Babe," says Kenny, "it's not like that. It's not, swear it. It's just a work thing is all."

"You think you're better than me, don't you? All fancy and shit, working for a doctor. You ain't shit, Kenny."

"Stop it. You're being ridiculous."

"Then why ain't I met any your work folks?"

"Because it's work, Martha. Work is for work and home is for home, alright?"

"Fuck you."

"Look," Kenny says, "I don't even have to go. I won't go. I'll stay right here with you, happy?"

Look at what Kenny's become. Just look at the man he is now. Look what Martha's done to him. But it isn't enough.

Kenny leaves for a week this time, but even if he hadn't, nothing would've changed.

~

Effect: Sudden Infant Death Syndrome.

~

Effect: Technically, three years old is a toddler, but it doesn't matter.

His toddler body is buried to the right of Little Jimmy. His toddler body is filled up with arsenic, too.

~

Effect: His firstborn son, his firstborn.

~

Effect: Years of submission and apology.

~

Affect: A house on mute.

~

Effect: Martha is the Queen. She rules. She is a dictator and everyone bows to her.

But there are only two of us left.

~

Affect: A halo instead of a crown.

MURDER NO. 4

Affect: Kenny locks the front door.

~

Effect: Forever.

~

Effect: 250 pounds of flesh licking flesh.

~

Effect: I am buried beside Suzie Ann. I am eleven years old.

~

Effect: I land here, not living.

~

Affect: A punishment that never ends.

~

Effect: A divorce.

AFTERMATH

Effect: The chair.
Effect: The cocktail.
Effect: Life without parole.
Effect: Freedom, gone forever.
Affect: What is freedom.
Effect: Just life, just life.

FROM BEHIND, FROM BEYOND

Today, Martha's celly catches chain so she has the place all to herself.

~

Today, Martha is exhausted. She's been laughing forever, it seems. She bellows, and there is no one around to hear her. There is no more television. She is all alone with her tray. She is chained to the wall. She has been a naughty girl, and it's just so funny. "Wham," she says, and she gets back to laughing again. She goes to slap her forehead, but the chain isn't long enough. It busts against her wrist, but nothing breaks, except her laughter—even that is only a fleeting pain.

~

Today, Martha is still in solitary.

~

Today, Martha is back in with the general population. Her new celly looks like she's still detoxing. She got the shakes bad, and she shits every two minutes.

"Fuck's wrong with you?" Martha says.

"Shush," the woman says. "They can always hear."

"No one hears nothing in here. No one cares."

And then something blows into Martha, something that resembles concern, it has the silhouette of warmth and love. It looks maternal. "You scared?" she asks.

"Keep off me you fat bitch."

"Pooey," Martha says. She pulls herself off the bed. Its cheap coils burn against the burden of her body. "Nothing can hurt you in here."

The woman pushes herself against the cinder block wall. Its white makes everything glow.

"Tell Martha what happened." She lets her fat hand fall onto the woman's head. It slides down to her shoulder and Martha rubs it. "Martha remembers she used to have a pretty girl just like you."

The woman breaks, just a little. "Yeah?"

"Yeah."

"She out in the free world?"

"No," Martha says. "She ain't nowhere anymore." Martha looks around the cell. It's small against the enormity of her body. "I remember, though. I sure do." Her arms make a cradle like she is holding something real nice.

"I got one too," the woman says. "She's still small. Ain't right that they don't let me have her no more."

"Sometimes, I think she's still here. She's in here. With me." Martha's eyes circle and they stop right on me. Two oceans, looking at me without knowing it. "She's right here still."

The woman reaches a hand out to Martha. They touch. "She ain't, mama. Just you and me in here."

"No," Martha says, "my baby girl's right here now. Bunny rabbit? You hear me?"

Everything dissolves: Martha, this woman, the prison, and when I can see again, I'm back here, with the dead and the helpless. I'm crying. My tears are quiet.

~

Today, Martha stirs gravy into her mashed potatoes.

~

Today, Martha puts green jello into her hand and smashes it. And then she eats it.

~

Today, her celly goes out for rec time, and Martha can't make herself get up.

~

Today, there is a fight, and Martha yells, "Whammy," and Martha yells, "Get her," and Martha yells, "Whammy whammy boo boo."

~

Today, Martha stands in front of a line of men and women in black suits and black guard suits. She says, "I'm real sorry for it."

~

The anger in her grooves like cancer. She isn't sick.

~

"Time for rec," the guard says.

"Ain't going," Martha says.

"Everyone's gotta go." The guard beats his hand against her open cell. "Up."

"Ain't going," Martha says.

"You don't go, you don't get a tray tonight."

Martha swings her legs off the bed, but they can't move. She's stuck there. "Ain't going," she says. "Go ahead and starve me."

"Ha," says the guard. "Fat chance."

~

Today, Martha is dreaming.

She is snoring and her eyelids crunch and release.

She rolls back and forth.

In sleep, she says, "Ahh," and then she grins. Her teeth are spotted brown.

THE MAKING OF MARTHA

SUMMER

A house becomes a home, covered in salmon adobe with three modest bedrooms and one full bathroom. The half-bath doesn't have any running water and is only for the looking. Underneath, it is composed of cheap cinder blocks. The floors are covered with dark beige honey-combed carpet, but stains are visible from every angle.

During the summer monsoons, the swamp cooler doesn't work and all the wooden components of the house swell. Swamp coolers are reliant on the dry air of the desert. Doors must be slammed, and even then, locks struggle to click into place.

~

Martha is still mourning. Erwin has been dead a few months, Suzie Ann not even a year gone. Martha wails for the injustice that falls on her neck, sharp as a guillotine blade and just as iron dense.

Martha points right at my face. "You did this. This is all your fault, don't you know?"

I am nine years old and my hair is cut short like a boy's. "Mama," I say.

"Shut your fucking hole."

Kenny is at work. He's always at work or somewhere else, anywhere else but here.

"Why?" Her voice trembles, it breaks. "Why'd you have to do it?"

I, too, feel a debt to sadness.

"Mama," I say. "I love—"

"As if you matter."

~

The monsoons mean that summer is almost over. They mean I maybe might escape Martha's tyranny for the daylight hours. In school, I am safe.

School is a fantasy.

The monsoons mean another month of imprisonment with Martha.

I write everything down in my diary and then I tear out every page. I burn them one by one and pour the ash into my mouth.

~

"What?"

"Can I," I whisper. My voice is tiny. "Can I go to—"

"What's that, girl? I can't hear you. How many times I got to tell you to talk normal?" Martha starts clapping. A guy with a stunning smile has just won big on *Press Your Luck*. "I don't want no whammies," Martha announces.

The lock on the door snaps and here's Kenny. He stinks. It doesn't matter where he's been. No one cares anymore.

"Hahahaha," bellows Martha. She sings, "Stupid got a whammy! Stupid got a whammy!"

Kenny slides down the hall like a shadow, and so he escapes another fiasco this time.

"Get me a bottle of Seagrams."

I open the refrigerator and look. There's just bottles in here and entire chocolate cakes, some bologna and a jar of mayonnaise. "What color?" I ask.

"You talking to yourself again, Arlene?"

"No ma'am. I was just asking you what color I can get you."

"They ain't colors, stupid. Strawberry daiquiri, and read the goddamn label, will you? Don't just bring me a red one or I'll slap you a good one for being lazy and dumb."

I turn all the bottles so the labels face forward. I count them three times. We're out of strawberry daiquiri. I pull out a red one and try to rub off the label. Most of it sticks on but the flavor part is just the white underneath. I pop open the top with a lighter and bring it to Martha.

"Come on," she says. "Get a whammy. Get a whammy." Martha stares at the screen. "I'll whammy you," she says and she kicks the top of her head toward me. The pretty girl on the screen peeps a little song of joy. She's bouncing and pumps her hands up. The audience claps and some of them even cheer.

Martha's face is red. She punches her thighs. "Get her," she says. "Get that bitch."

She spins the wheel again.

~

This is the summer that I see the Barnum and Bailey circus on television. Afterwards, I pretend I am flying acrobat. I tie a scarf around my neck and swing from the ceiling fan. Eventually, I fall to the ground, and there is no safety net. There is no buoyancy to my fall.

~

Ana comes over every day and asks if I can go to play, but we both know that Martha would never let me. Even when I am brave enough to ask, it's all for nothing.

"No dice?" Ana asks.

"Nah," I say. "I'm sorry."

"It's cool," and then Ana hops on her Schwinn and rides off to play with someone who isn't me.

FALL

This is the only kind of fall the house has known: hot and mildly hot. The leaves stay indignantly green. There is little to notice in this change in season. But the house has heard rumors of other places, places where technicolor leaves imprint joy onto the roofs of houses far, far away, rumors of crispy breezes and even snow. But those are only rumors of places the house has never seen. The house doesn't believe in magic stories, fairy tales for little kids. The house knows better.

Instead, the house waits for the temperature to settle down enough to cover the swamp cooler for the year. The windows will all be opened and maybe that will soothe the anger that is housed inside the house.

For all the house has seen, it continues to hope.

~

It's a Wednesday night in late September. I have the back door open to invite the cool air in, and I'm sitting at the kitchen table sweating and doing homework. Martha went to the store and Kenny's never here, so I'm enjoying a can of orange Crush all by myself.

"I bet there's no one home at this one." It's a man's voice and it's moving fast.

"Man, there's a fucking light on. Can't you see that?"

"So?"

"So what?"

"So what, what?"

"Shut up, man. Don't confuse me. Focus now. Focus." There are three slaps. The first two are light and fast, the final draws in air both ways.

The metal gate opens and closes.

"Fucking be quiet."

Someone jumps.

"It's under there," in a frantic whisper.

"You're just making it worse, man. There's nothing there. I'm looking right at you and there's nothing there." Another slap, this one severe. "Stop scratching your fucking face already, OK? You're just making it worse. There ain't nothing down there, you hear me?"

By the time they get to the door, I'm not scared anymore.

I stand up and look at their faces. I say, "You can kill me if you want." I say, "I won't even scream, I promise."

When Martha gets home, everything is quiet again.

~

"Arlene! Get in here and help me!"

"Coming!" I put a pencil in to mark the page and close the book. "I'm coming right away."

In the living room, Martha is rocking back and forth on her recliner. "Get over here now."

I scramble my way toward her. I anchor my feet to the ground. "OK," I say. "I'm ready."

Martha grabs hold of my shoulder, and she tries to pull herself up. She falls back.

"One more time." I gird my body.

My back bends and her weight is enormous.

~

I dream that they slit my throat and it's a quick death. It almost feels good. It doesn't even hurt that much because it's like all the hurt from inside me can swim out with my blood.

When I wake up, I begin to learn all I can about leeches and the relief they can give—and cutting, too.

~

We are driving to Hatch for the Green Chile Festival. Kenny is behind the wheel and I'm his copilot. Martha has her legs kicked up. She takes the whole back seat and all the air around it, too.

"Change it," she says. She makes as if to reach in the space between Kenny and me, but I go to click the button to change the station myself because I don't want her dividing us, Kenny and me and our closeness. Besides, I know it's just a gesture. Martha doesn't think she's going to do anything. She doesn't need to. That's why I'm here, to serve her.

Tejano music comes through.

"Change it."

Mozart's trills.

"Change it.

"—news story for you, wow. A woman suffocated her two—" A news announcer. I change the button before I'm told to.

"Goddamn it," Kenny says and he turns off the radio. He slaps the steering wheel. "We're here."

~

"Come sit." Martha nods to the empty spot next to her on the bench. "You're gonna like this, Arlene. Yeah, yeah, you're gonna like it a whole lot."

Women in dark green gowns stride around the makeshift stage. It's unusually cold, and I can see goose pimples on all of their tan shoulders and down into their small wrists.

"Oh, look at that one Arlene," and then, "Look at that one," and then, "Oh, look there, Arlene. Isn't it so pretty? Ain't it just so pretty?"

We leave before the queen is crowned.

"This way," Martha says, "all of them win equally, and that means no one wins. When there's no loser, winning is empty."

~

"Hey Kenny," I say as casually as I can.

"There's my girl." Kenny opens up one arm for me to fit in for a hug. He's sitting at the kitchen table, just drinking coffee and looking at the calendar on the wall. "This stupid thing thinks it's still summer."

The time for Erwin's funeral is written beneath the square of the date. It's my handwriting.

I go over and pull of sheet after sheet until it's finally October. I fold up the pages into neat squares and throw them into the trash-can. "Hey, can I ask you something?" I'm looking down into the garbage in case Kenny rejects me.

He comes over and hugs me.

"What's gonna happen next?" I ask.

I wish we could stay close like this forever.

~

When my friends come over to play, we stay outside. I don't let them go in. They don't want to anyway. We all know what's inside. We know what's happened in there.

And—we know that's the same place I have to sleep every night.

Even though it's late fall, it's hot as guts outside.

"Let's go somewhere else," Lluvia says. "It's way too freaking hot."

Lluvia, Ana, and I are playing house but there's not really a house anywhere. We had pulled a sheet over all the prickly pears in my backyard and crawled underneath the canopy. Lluvia's right. It's way too freaking hot.

"Well," Lluvia says, "I guess *we* could somewhere, but I doubt *you* could go, am I right?"

And Ana says, "Don't be mean. We should all go or not."

My feelings are bruised but I pretend they're not.

"It's OK," I say. "You guys don't have to stay here. It's pretty hot."

"No way," Ana says. "I'm not going anywhere. Not without you."

The only clean sheet I could find was a dark gray fitted one. It takes in all the sunlight and it feels like an oven in here.

But Lluvia goes, "We could go to my apartment. We've got refrigerated air."

And Ana goes, "Man, that *does* sound pretty nice right now."

"Of course it does," I go. I go, "My house is a bummer."

"Do you think you could come too?"

"Of course she can't. Don't be a dummy."

And of course I can't. Martha will never let me.

After they leave, I run my palms against the cactus stem. They look smooth, but there are spines hidden—almost invisible—in the areoles.

WINTER

Cinder blocks are not adobe and in the winter, the house is often chilly. Not cold or freezing, but the house wishes it could cover itself with a shawl. Nothing too heavy, maybe a light silk. By midday, its walls absorb the sun, and the house wishes it could just bake all day long. Besides, what else would it have to do?

And so the house lounges in the sun, right where it is, going nowhere, wanting to go nowhere, totally content. The house feels content.

~

"Arlene," Martha calls.

"Coming!" I hurry off the bed. "I'm coming right now."

It's still morning and there are bottles all over the living room: on the end tables, on the carpet, I see one tucked between the folds of the sofa.

"I'm hungry. Go get me something to eat."

"Um."

"What's your problem? You deaf now or what? I said go get me something to eat."

"But how?"

"How what? Get out of here and don't go coming back till you have food for me."

"Yes ma'am."

I go back into my room and close the door. I lift my mattress and pull out a ten dollar bill. Wendy's isn't too far, and it's not like I haven't walked there a million times before. I should have enough money to get her a double cheeseburger with bacon and a large fries and a large Frosty, and maybe that'll make her happy.

I don't really care if I make Martha happy.

I don't need her to love me.

I just need to endure enough to hope I survive.

~

When Martha forgets to give me lunch money, I just don't eat. When there's no food in the house except cake, I just don't eat. We never have breakfast here unless Kenny is home. I don't need to eat. Not really, not ever.

~

"Hey Kenny," I say. I'm sitting in the kitchen doing homework.

"There's my girl. What you doing?"

"Homework."

"Oh Arlene, even your pants are smart."

Kenny laughs and then I laugh too and we are laughing together. It feels so full that it might never end.

From the other room, "No whammy," chants from the television and out of Martha's mouth. It's the only sound the house contains. Our laughter is spent.

~

This is the winter I learn to sew. Martha says I'm a fat slut who doesn't deserve new shit, but my coat is too small for me and so are my mittens.

Winters someplace else are meant for hibernation, but in New Mexico, we just keep on waiting for tomorrow. In the Land of Mañana, tomorrow, things will happen. Tomorrow, there will be sun, sunshine for days and days, a whole lifetime of sunshine. Even though it's winter, I am warm enough. I don't need anything else. I say to Martha, "Yes ma'am, you're right."

"Just shut it already," she says. "Can't you see I'm busy?"

I do.

~

Pricks of blood rise to my fingertips. I like the way it tastes, how hard I have to pull with my teeth, how my skin softens from all that spit.

Finally, the thread scoops through the eye of the needle.

~

The family inside has never used the fireplace. Smoke has not risen through the house's chimney for too long. Even the house is surprised by how much it misses the feel of soot.

~

"Aren't you hungry?" Ana asks me. It's lunch, and I'm sitting between Ana and Lluvia. Tomas and Mikey are here, too. I think Mikey is cute, but he probably still thinks girls are gross.

"Nah," I say. "I had a big breakfast."

Lluvia fake laughs. "Uh-huh, I'm sure you did." Her voice is sly like Vaseline.

"Here," Ana says. She pushes her tray of green enchiladas at me. "I wanted a cheeseburger anyway."

"I don't need this."

"I know." Her voice is serious. "But please just eat it for me?"

~

Tonight, Mars is red in the night sky. Its tinting is slight, but everyone outside here can see it: me, Kenny, just us two. Martha is inside the house. Sometimes, I wish the house could see, that the house might care, that it could somehow save me, but that's ridiculous.

The sky is so enormous. All those stars up there have planets circling them. Our sun isn't even that big, not in comparison. Its scale is beyond what my brain can handle. I've never seen anything so huge. It's bigger than my imagination can stretch.

"What do you think about aliens?" I ask.

I adjust my scarf because the wind is picking up a little. I zip up my hoodie. It's too cold for this type of jacket, but I can only use what I have.

"Well," says Kenny, "that's a complicated question, you see, because we live on the border so I think they should get the fuck out but I also want them here to wash the dishes."

"Kenny? I meant the aliens in the sky." I point up.

"Well, shit. Sorry." He scratches at that line between hair and neck. "You think they're real?"

We both look at the sky. The moon is half-full and half of that is covered by thin black clouds. Light falls in striations.

"I don't know. I mean, I guess with all those worlds out there, there must be other things like us. Well, maybe not exactly like us like us, but thinking, like us."

"Do you think heaven is in outer space?"

"Geez, Arlene," he says, "deep questions over here."

"I just mean," I think carefully, "we don't believe in God or anything, but what if when we died, we didn't die but instead we just went up to space somewhere. I mean, there's so much space up there being useless. What if we used just some of it? Not all of it, but some of it."

"We'd be dead though, sweetheart."

Between us, the air wiggles around. It dances and we move closer together. I whisper, "It's gonna happen sometime. Can't stop it, Kenny. No one can stop her."

"I like what you're saying, Arlene." Kenny's voice is loud like either he's ignoring what I just said or that he didn't hear it at all. "I mean, yeah, I'd never thought about it before, but why couldn't we go to space after we died? I mean, I can't really think of a reason why not."

I'm glad that it's so dark out here because my emotions can stay hidden. I choke a little. "Yeah," I say. "Why not?"

~

"Arlene!" Martha is calling. She's always calling. I leave my book face down on the bed with the pages open and I hate the way the spine bends, its flexibility.

"Coming," I say. "I'm coming right now."

"Wheel! Of!" Martha looks over at me. "Get me some cake."

I run to the kitchen. I open the fridge and take out half of a chocolate cake. I bring it to Martha with a fork and a paper towel.

"Where's the fucking whipping cream? You know I like whipping cream with this."

But there is no whipping cream. I had looked, and there's none. "I'm sorry," I say, "but there's none here."

"Well?"

"I'm sorry ma'am."

"I'm setting the clock. You got ten minutes to get back here." Martha sets the timer on the coffee table. She likes to have one handy.

SPRING

As the sun crests the Organ Mountains, there is still a sliver of red moon up in the sky. The colors are blazing pastels, color everything: pinks and oranges, shades in between and exceeding. The beauty here is excessive.

The house likes the mornings most of all. The rising sun calls the flowers to lift their petals. They open their buds and extend on up, toward the warmth and toward nourishment.

The days are starting to get longer, and the winds are extravagant in March. Dust swallows people riding bicycles and the leaves just beginning to pop out of the branches of trees. It slides into the cracks of every house, and the floors are dirty and plain.

~

I love to spring forward, how days open wider. My circumstances never change, but at least there are fewer shadows for the monster to hide in.

She doesn't want to hide though.

She doesn't need to.

She is a monster, even under the broad umbrella of daylight.

~

The doctor tells Kenny that there's something wrong with me.

"You're just a little worrier, aren't you, Arlene?"

I'm in the office where Kenny works. He talks to the doctor like they're old friends. There's a poster up about blood flow and diabetes. There are brochures about brain sickness and different ways to cure it.

"I'm sorry," I say.

"What are you worrying about? You're too young for this kind of thing."

"Oh," I say. "School is just stressful. That's all." I look at Kenny who looks at me and then the doctor.

"It'll still be—" he stops for a second, scratches at his neck, "difficult." His eyes cloud over. "You know, at home and all."

After we go to the pharmacy, Kenny buys me a milkshake and we sit under a mulberry tree that is just beginning to become fragrant with flower.

~

For Spring Break, Lluvia invites Ana to go with her and her family to Tucson for vacation. Ana comes back with a ton of pictures of the resort they stayed in. There was a double winding slide with a jet of water that twirls them right into the deep end of the bluest pool I've ever seen.

Martha wouldn't have let me go anyway.

Lluvia didn't invite me, so it doesn't matter either way.

~

Missus Gomez tries to call Martha in because she's worried about me. She says it's my homework. She says it's not normal.

She sends me home with a note.

"Here," I say, holding the piece of paper out to Martha. I've already read it, and I know that Martha doesn't care enough to do anything.

"What is it?"

"It's a note," I say. "From my teacher. She wants to see you."

"What the fuck'd you do this time?"

"Nothing ma'am. It's just time for parent-teacher conferences is all."

Martha stops looking at the television and puts her eyes on me. "You ain't lying to me now is you?"

"No ma'am." I start to unfold the paper for her to read it. This is all for show.

"Hahahaha." Martha guffaws. On the screen, the man in a hunter green polo has just landed on Bankrupt. "Fucker, that's what you get."

"Do you want to read it?" This is a game. If she ever called my bluff, it'd turn out real bad for me, but I know Martha doesn't care about me so it doesn't matter.

The next day, my teacher will send me home with another note, this one about the obvious forgery of the previous day's note.

I will not bother Martha with it.

I will sign it again, this time with Kenny's signature and it will look like an exact copy of the real thing.

~

Dew makes everything slick and shiny in the morning. There are tiny optical illusions in the waiting.

The house stretches in condensation and sighs it all out when the clouds shade the blueberry sky.

~

"Get in here," Martha yells.

"Coming," I say. "I'm coming there right away." I put my book into my backpack and zip it closed. I throw a blanket on top of the whole thing.

The television isn't moving. There's a woman midspin, her arms lifted above her head and the wheel glistens. Her dress is without contour but it's clear she's all curves under there.

"Fix," Martha says.

"But I don't know how." And quickly, I add, "I'm sorry."

"Yeah you do, you little shit." Martha's eyes narrow. "Fucking get it done."

"But I—"

"Shut up shut up shut up!"

"I'm—"

"Shut up shut up shut up!"

"I'm sorry. I'll go fix it now. I'm so sorry."

~

I miss a step climbing onto our flat-top roof, but I don't fall. I guess every idea has to start somewhere.

I twist the antenna. I turn it. I stand as close to the edge as possible.

I don't cry out. Martha wouldn't do anything anyway. I can hear her calling me from the living room, but my body hurts too much to care.

Kenny finds me a few hours later and he drives me to the emergency room because it's an emergency.

There's a needle and suddenly it doesn't hurt anymore. My muscles feel warm.

This is bliss. Later, they will give me a bottle to stop the pain at home and every time I swallow a pill, I can come back here.

But the pain at home is not caused by my broken body, and bliss shatters every three or four hours. I take more because I have to. I double the dose for a chance at escape.

~

Ana invites me and Lluvia over for Easter Sunday and an egg hunt. Her mama makes a big ham and potato salad and tamales. We girls each get a basket full of chocolate bunnies, all of which I give to Ana in secret, and yellow marshmallow chicks, which I like a lot. Everything is set atop plastic green grass.

This is the best Easter I've ever had.

Before this, I didn't know about Easter, except from books.

The pastel eggs are beautiful. The confetti inside them goes all over the place when we crack those shells on the top of each other's heads and run for cover!

~

And yes, there is the day that I line them all up.

First, I puke, then I sleep and I wish I would never wake up but of course I do.

Martha says, "I been calling you all day. You deaf or what?"

"I'm sorry ma'am." There is crust along my eyes. They can barely open.

"So?"

"I'm sorry ma'am," I say.

"I says where you been girl?"

Everything is revolting and bright. I run to the toilet, and when I'm done, I don't feel any better at all.

~

Spring is a time for cleaning, for cleansing and purging.

The house has not been swept in years.

During the windy season, the house claps shut its eyes. It cannot even breathe.

SUMMER

It's absurd, this heat. It just climbs up and up. It doesn't soften, even in the night. The house groans and then it exhales with a pout. The paint on the adobe falls off in clumps. Everything is getting older: the house's bones, its inner organs, even its skin. The years keep on accumulating and no one cares about the house. No one has ever cared for it. Sometimes, it feels lonesome and abandoned, even when it is full of people. But the people inside don't know love. How could they? Such ugliness in there, inside it, occupying it, and so the house only knows about the boldness of avarice and artificial tenderness of murder. Gluttony emboldens these walls; revenge cracks open the floors. Summer is crowning, but the little girl in the house still wears socks. She is a weak one and only getting weaker. The house would like to do something to help her, it really does, but what can a house do? It just watches and everything keeps going wrong. It always does.

And so the stalwart house weeps.

~

Ana's mom just moved to an apartment on the nice side of town, but her dad still lives by me. She doesn't come back that often anymore. Lluvia gets to go over there all the time, but Martha never lets me.

Martha can't really get up now without my help. She can't do anything without my help.

She's useless and I hate her.

And she keeps on getting fatter.

I'm hungry, but I don't need to eat. I never want to eat again.

~

"Goddamn it!"

"Coming," I say. I burn up the last of the diary entry and shove it in my mouth. Even though it's ash, it's still hot. It doesn't hurt that much. "I'm coming right now."

Martha's watching her soaps. She likes to call them her "dopes" and then she always laughs about it. All the commercials are for cleaning houses, things that make a woman a good wife. Martha is not a good wife.

"Yes ma'am. I'm here."

"Fuck took so long?" Martha is eating chocolate cake with her fingers. Her nails have a film of oily brown sheen all over them.

"I'm sorry. I was just—"

She isn't a good mother, either.

"Just shut up then. Why you got to talk so damn much all the time?"

"I—"

"What you mean, you little shit, is that you was just going to get me some ice cream to go along with this cake." Martha puts a large chunk in the palm of her hand and stuffs the whole thing into her mouth. "And don't you go thinking any funny shit neither."

"I'm sorry ma'am."

"Yeah? For what?"

A bald man promises the cleanest floors ever. There's a wink in his smile.

"I'll go to the store now."

The hourglass does not need to rotate. It doesn't need any extra dramatic effect.

"Arlene," Martha says.

"Yes ma'am. I'm here. I'm still right here."

She doesn't look at me. She never sees my eyes.

~

Lluvia comes over and is like, "Too bad you're not going to the same school as me and Ana next year."

"Yeah," I say.

"It's like, who's even gonna be your friend there?"

"I dunno." I start kicking at the dirt in my yard. I'm sweating and it pools around my neck. It slides down thickly.

"You know, Ana's like your only friend. Like, in the world."

I lift my shirt to wipe the sweat from my forehead.

"That's gross," Lluvia says, and then she's like, "No one wants to see your titties that aren't even there yet."

"Sorry," I say. I don't know what I'm sorry for. It's just something I say because I know I'm always wrong.

"You're like way too skinny."

"I dunno."

"It's like ugly on you, and it's not that I'm jealous of you or something because I'm not. Like at all. You know what the other kids call you?"

"No."

"They call you—"

"Wait," I say. "I don't wanna know."

"I'm talking. Don't be rude."

"Sorry."

"What was I just saying? Oh, yeah, they call you—"

"No," I yell. "Don't tell me. I don't want to know, OK?" I shove her and she falls down.

"You bitch," Lluvia says. She grabs a handful of dirt and throws it at me. "Just wait till I tell Ana about this. She's gonna hate you and she's never gonna talk to you again."

She spits at me, but I dart away just in time.

"Like ever ever ever again." She throws another clump of dirt at me, and this one hits me square in the arm.

I run inside and go straight to the toilet.

When I flush, I feel clean again, but it feels terrible.

~

When I imagine my future life, when I lack enough wits to have hope, I'm married to man named Jonathan and he's successful and handsome and we don't have any children, but we love each other a lot. Maybe his name is Michael or Joshua or Paul, nothing too strange, because ours will be a normal life. No drama and no one dies. We live forever and our house is always laughing along with us.

He does something professional and so do I. I think I would like to be a neurosurgeon or a social worker, but his job is always better than mine. He's a banker or maybe a lawyer.

We have a perfect life. There are no babies, and so no babies ever die. They live forever because I have not loved them. If I love a baby, it dies, so Jonathan or Joshua or Michael or Paul and I will have the best life ever.

I write out his name and draw a big heart around it.

~

It's so hot and Martha won't let me go to the pool to swim. "Fucking waste of money," she says, and she could mean the pool just as much as she could mean me.

It doesn't matter anyway because I never learned how to swim.

Instead, I fill up the tub with cold water and hold my breath for as long as I can. I'm always disappointed when I cough the water out of my lungs.

My swimsuit sticks to my skin when I get out, but it's not really a swimsuit. Just some panties and a big t-shirt. Everything is just a fucking waste of money.

~

There's no babies left, only me and Martha and Kenny.

Will Kenny still love her after I'm dead?

I want to tell him that he can't, that he has to get away, but every time I try, I have to run away before I start crying all over the place. I'm too old now to go around crying. Besides, what would it even do?

~

Over the phone, Ana says, "I miss you, Arlene."

"I miss you too," I say back.

"Vivi told me."

"Vivi?"

"Um, Lluvia?"

"Oh, of course."

I turned eleven last month and now my armpits stink. There's hair there now. It's gross but there's nothing I can do to stop becoming a werewolf.

"She's mean," I say.

"I wish you could come over. The pool's real nice here."

"Me too."

"Oh, hey, gotta go," she says. "Vivi's here."

"Wait," I say, but she's already hung up. It's just a buzzing now, a monotone song to replace her graceful voice.

~

When it cools down at night, I go up to the roof. The stars are closer up there, but even the moon is sweating. The swamp cooler kicks on and the house shifts. I imagine that it's sighing.

Jupiter's out tonight, a lavender sparkle right next to Venus. A star falls and I make a wish. Up there, alone, I cry because there's nothing left to do. There's not a single witness, and I wish she would just kill me already.

~

The house wishes it could contract its walls and hug the little girl. She's so sad and afraid.

The house wishes it could contract its walls and crush the little girl's mother.

The house wishes it could enact justice.

But a house is only a house. It's immobile and helpless.

It can't do anything at all.

~

"Kenny," Martha calls. "Get your ass in here."

I'm standing next to her and she can't get up not matter now hard she pushes down on me.

Kenny rushes in.

"Give the girl a twenty," she says.

Kenny pulls open his wallet. "I only have seventeen dollars."

"That's enough."

He hands me the money.

School starts in a week and all of my clothes are too small.

"Get me an ice cream cake. The green one."

She pushes deep into my shoulder. Martha falls back into the sofa. "Fucking worthless." She points at my face and then she looks at Kenny. "Git," she says and we both hurry our way toward freedom.

THE FALL

The house never notices the onset of fall, but before long, the leaves turn crispy. Life clutters out and away, and sometimes, the colors even change. It's not a blushing like a shy school girl. No, more like the way skin browns from too much sun and wrinkles crack everywhere. It's a drying out. A lack of proper nutrition. It's death. Lucky, lucky, leaves aren't like the babies that used to live inside the house. For those babies, death is forever and there is no more spring, no more budding, no more anything. Just nothing else—ever.

By midseason, the house whistles and rejoices the cooling air.

By late-season, the house shivers in the witching hours, the hours right before the sun breaks. Those are the coldest hours, the loneliest, too.

~

Ana only gets one weekend a month with her dad, so he rarely lets her go out and play. Sometimes, she sneaks out at night to see me. Sometimes. Other times, I can go for two or three months without seeing her even once.

Every time I see her, our bodies have changed. Become less girlish. Curves appear and hair. Mounds come up from our chests and push at our skin and grow. It's not bad, but it sure hurts.

Our conversations turn into obsessions over boys and calories and Ana is a pretty girl. She hangs out with the eighth graders, and I know that if we went to the same middle school, I wouldn't be cool enough for her time. Not anymore.

"Arlene." A fingernail scratches at my window. "You up?"

I'm not but I shake the sleep from my voice best I can and say, "That you, Ana?"

"Course it is," she says. "You waiting on some boy in my place? Ohh, you are! I know you are. Spill it. Who is he?"

"Oh, I dunno. I guess I was really hoping it was Sam." I don't know any guy named Sam. Any girl either for that matter.

I open the window all the way for her to get in. There's a chair on my side for when she hoists her body through. It's a landing.

"Which one's Sam again?" Ana says. "So many I can't keep them straight." She twirls some hair around her forefinger, clearly trying to make fun of me even though I've never done a hair twirl, never: not my thing.

"You wanna go to the arroyo?" Ana is whispering. We both know that Martha is out cold, but there's always the chance she isn't. We don't know what would happen if she caught Ana in here or if she woke up and I wasn't here for her, but gambles are gambles and sometimes the house doesn't win.

"You mean," I fluff up my hair and push my belly as far out as it can go, "the ditch?" I'm making fun of Lluvia. Now that she's fat, no one is friends with her. Not even Ana. Or me, obviously.

"You're so bad," Ana says. Then she extends her belly out, too, and says, "That ditch is, like, such a waste." She stomps over like a monster and our buttons touch. This is closeness, this is something that could last forever but of course I know that's impossible. Friends are people who change—and some of them just end up dead.

We chuckle together and then hold in our laughs because we don't want to wake the beast, but then Ana chokes on it and out comes the laugh of a joyful hyena. She's so loud, so accidentally loud, that everything is funnier, and we both jump onto the chair and out the window and then we both laugh all the way to the path that takes us to the magic arroyo. It's our special place. We go there late at night, when the rest of Las Cruces is sleeping, and there's no light there, just the moon blinking in the clear black sky. When the moon is full, the darkness is flushed and the stones illuminate, but tonight, the moon is waning and we can barely see the path. We hold hands, in case one of us falls down. Everything between us is different now, but things are still the same, too.

"Oh oh oh girl," goes Ana. "Did I tell you about Ray yet?"

"Maybe, I don't know. Which one is he?"

"He's a freshman. In high school! He plays varsity even though he's still a freshman. He's not a fancy position or anything. I think he's on defense so he tackles big guys all day. He's got muscles forever."

"Wow," I say. I'm genuinely amazed. We are in sixth grade, just starting out middle school, and already, Ana's being courted by a high school boy, and not just some plain boy, he's on varsity. He's a catch no matter what.

"Yeah," she says. And, "And can you believe it? He asked me—me!—to go with him to the Fall Ball!"

"Wow," I say again. It's starting to sound stupid now, or, maybe like I don't believe her or something.

"Like a real high school dance."

"You said yes, right?"

"Well," she says. Her voice is flat and this is how I know she is being serious and not just girl chattering anymore. "Actually, I got scared so I told him I'd need to think about it. Age gap and all. And can you believe it? He said something smooth about how it's just a number and I'm something special, he can see it just when he looks at me."

"Ana," I say, "you know you have to go. I mean, at least for me. "No high school boy is ever going to ask me to a dance, so please, for me, you just need to go!"

Sadly, that's going to be a true statement, but I doubt I knew it back then but maybe I did.

I say, "So are you really thinking about it or did you just say that?"

"It's kind of a big deal, you know? It'd be my first dance ever and maybe high school is still too scary for me. I mean, he's kinda out of my league already."

"That's like not even possible."

"He's super hot and cute. He gets bad grades and all but I know he's smart. He just doesn't try is all."

"So you really are thinking about it?"

"Yeah right," Ana goes. "Of course I'm going, but I can't make it out like I'm super excited about it or anything. Even though I am, like duh."

"You're so smart, Ana. You always know exactly what to do."

A star falls. It's a dim one, but it's beautiful.

~

"What the fuck is—"

"I'm sorry ma'am." Apologies just run out of my mouth, when I mean them, when I don't. It's all the same with Martha.

"Just shut up."

"Yes ma'am."

The man on the television spins the large wheel. He looks tall, but the wheel is taller. The numbers are laced with glitter.

Suddenly, everything scrambles and then it stops moving altogether.

"What the—"

"I'm sorry," I say.

"Shut your goddamn trap and fix it."

"I'm—"

"If you says you sorry one more time, I swear it's gonna be your end."

I swallow and say nothing. I apologize but only in my head.

The man is midjump. The wheel is caught on one hundred. His arms are lifted above his head, and his extended muscles are golden.

"No, no, no. Fix this." She points at the screen with the remote control. "Git your ass on the roof and fix this. You dumb? I had to tell you to fix this twice, and if I gots to say it even one more—"

"Yes ma'am. Yes of course I'm going. I'm going right now."

~

I push the step ladder next to the wall and I have to scale the chimney and jump in order to make it onto the roof. Getting up isn't that hard, but getting down is much trickier. I twist the antennae this way and that, but what I want to do most is break the thing. I want to snap it into a thousand metal pieces and throw them all at Martha.

Instead, I fall.

I fall into the air and through it.

I'm not scared; this is my escape.

~

"There's my girl," Kenny says.

"Kenny? That you?" Everything is sullen and gray. My body feels shattered.

"How you feeling?" I can feel his hand on my head. He's stroking my hair, and his hand must be made of stone or iron, but I don't want his touch to go away.

"Is Martha here?"

Kenny shakes his head. "You know how hard it is for her."

"Yeah," I say. "I'm glad."

"Arlene—"

"It's OK, Kenny. It's just, I'm glad it's just you and me is all."

"You want some water?" He looks around. "You must be thirsty. Let me get you some water."

"No, please. Don't leave me. Don't go." I'm desperate and he can hear it. I can hear it, too, because it's the way I really feel.

"It's OK sweetheart. I'm not going anywhere, OK? I'm right here. Kenny's not leaving you, not even for a millisecond."

Suddenly, there's a flame going wild inside my bones. I cry out.

"What is it? What it is, Arlene?"

I can't talk. I can't see. Nothing works.

And then—warmth slips through my body. It cuddles me. I'm safe now. "Kenny?"

"Just sleep, Arlene, just close your eyes and sleep. I'm not going anywhere. I'm gonna be right here for you." He keeps stroking my hair, but his hand is light now, like a breeze. It's just me and Kenny and we're floating off. Martha's gone, and we're just going to float all the way to Venus. "That's it sweetheart. Just—"

~

"—hurts too much, just press the button, OK sweetie? Show me you can press the button by yourself." The woman's voice is silver.

I do, and there is a sun inside me and it isn't hiding.

~

"Arlene? Sweetheart, wake up."

"Kenny?" I press the button. Everything becomes warm again.

"There she is." His smile makes everything bright. "This nice lady is here to talk to you, OK? Nothing's wrong. Don't worry none. She just wants to talk to you, but you've got to stay awake, OK? Can you do that for Kenny?"

I nod and it's too much. I press the button. I press it again.

"Hi Arlene, my name is Miss Anita. How are you feeling?"

"I'm sorry. I don't know what happened."

"You fell off the roof, Arlene, but it's OK. I just want to know how it happened."

"I'm sorry."

"Oh sweetheart," Kenny says. "There's nothing to be sorry about."

"I'm sorry."

"It's OK, Arlene. I'm just here to help." There's a sadness to the woman's voice. There's an echo that follows it. This is a nice woman. "Can you remember what happened?"

But there's no one to lift my sadness. I press the button.

"I went up to fix the TV, and I dunno what else next."

"How did you get up there?"

"I climbed."

"Do you go up there a lot?"

"Sometimes."

"Were you trying to hurt yourself?"

"No," I say. "I was just listening to Martha."

"And who's Martha?"

"She's my wife," says Kenny very quickly. "And Arlene's mama."

I say, "She's a monster."

"Arlene." Kenny's voice is solid.

"Why do you say she's a monster?"

I press the button because I don't know what to say next.

~

"It's not impossible."

"But you're not sure?"

"We'll just have to wait and see. It's not going to be an easy road for her. The damage was substantial."

The room is dark, but light makes it through all the cracks. There are cracks everywhere, so the light buzzes.

"You have to understand the seriousness of the injuries she sustained."

"I understand."

"Where's her mother?"

"Um—she's at home."

"The nurses tell me it's just been you here with her."

"Yeah."

But I'm not afraid of the light. I'm not afraid of the dark now, either. I don't have to be afraid because Martha isn't here.

"You're a good man, Kenny."

I agree. I agree with the whole of my body that isn't even whole anymore. When I close my eyes, colors twirl and spin.

~

"Hey Arlene."

"Ana?" My eyes can't focus. "I can't see you. I can't see anything." I press the button. "Why can't I see anything?" I press the button again. "Ana? Kenny? Kenny!" There's no button. There's nothing in my hand. "Kenny!" My hand, I can't feel my hand. "Please!"

"I'm here Arlene. Sorry I was just in the bathroom for a minute, but I'm here. I'm right here."

"Hold my hand. I can't feel anything. Why can't I feel anything? Kenny? Kenny!"

"It's OK, Arlene. It's gonna be OK. I'm just going to get a nurse, OK? Just don't freak out. It's all going to be OK."

"No don't go, Kenny please don't go." I want to reach out and grab him and hug him and keep him close to me but I can't do anything. I can't move anything. My body is a black hole.

"Shh, sweetheart, I'm not going anywhere. I'm right—Oh thank God you're here. It's my daughter, please, help us."

"Help me, please help me. I can't see and I can't move and I don't know what's going on. What's happening to me?"

"It's OK, Arlene. Just listen to my voice. Take a deep breath. Can you do that for me sweetie?"

I try to breathe in, but the air is made of needles. I scream out. "It hurts! It hurts! Help, Kenny, please."

And then—the sun comes back into my body. It burns, but I can feel it in there. I can feel again.

~

"Hey Arlene, sweetheart. Ana's here to see you."

"Ana? Is it you?"

"Hey Arlene."

"Hey."

"Thanks for coming again. I'm sorry about before. I hope I didn't scare you."

"Um—"

"Yeah, Ana, you came this morning, remember?" Kenny says.

"Oh, yeah, right. My mom drove me here. I just—it's just, I had a big math test today."

I start crying. I know I'm crying but the tears aren't really coming down my face. I know they're not. They're just stuck behind my eyes and all over them. Everything looks polished. It's all aura. "I mean it. Thanks for coming. It's real nice of you."

"Of course," Ana says, and her voice is broken. "I would've come earlier, I mean, earlier than this morning, but—"

"It just matters that you're here now."

"Oh Arlene, what happened?"

"I dunno."

"Hey, Kenny? Can I talk to Arlene for a minute by myself? You know, girl stuff?"

"No! Kenny, don't go."

"It's OK, Arlene. I'm here." Her voice is so soft. It can't remember if it's always been that way, but it's a lullaby. "Here," Ana says. "Hold my hand."

"Will you press the button for me?"

Solarian wind rushes into my blood and all over.

"Tell me what happened. What is Martha?"

"Are you holding my hand?"

"Yeah," she says. "Can't you feel it?"

"No," I say. "I haven't felt anything for I dunno how long."

"I'm sorry, Arlene. I'm just so sorry."

"Just don't leave me. Promise me you'll never leave me—"

"Of course! I'm never ever going to leave you again. Pinky swear."

I don't feel a thing.

"Will you press the button again?" Snowflakes made of sun rays gather along my spine. "You wanna go to Venus with me?"

"We can go wherever you want."

"Promise?"

"Oh Arlene. I can't believe this is—"

When night falls on the sun, everything stays bright.

MARTHA SEEKS REVENGE

Days become months and nothing heals with time. Martha rules the house, and Kenny no longer demands anything of her. He is a broken man now. More than my broken back, he's severe. He cowers and cries. He never argues. He pays tribute to Martha with his whole paycheck, and then he retreats into hiding. Away from her view, he is safe.

It takes me months to return home, and it wasn't long enough. I wasn't ready. I would never be ready, not to go back there, that gruesome place. It's cursed.

Kenny buys me a wheelchair because the doctors say even a miracle can't do all the fixing I need. No one wants to be my friend at school, when I go to school, which is almost never. They call me *retard.* They say I'm the *failed suicide queen.* I don't need to correct them. I wouldn't know what to say. I don't need to list out all the ways they're wrong—and right. Talk is useless to a girl who can't ever be saved.

~

Now neither Martha nor I can stand up on our own. Martha stays on her lazy boy, and I remain reclined on my bed all day. At night, if Kenny comes home, he pulls me upright and some nights he forgets to put me back down.

MEAL NO. 1: BREAKFAST

I can hear the crank of the sifter, and Martha bangs her hand against its cheap tin side. She is baking a cake. I know it isn't for me. It's always only for her.

Martha cracks an egg. She whisks it in.

The electric mixer comes alive and twirls and it spins.

Martha sets the timer and there's not a clock in my room.

When it chimes, she opens the oven door.

All I hear is chewing.

~

I'm not hungry, so it doesn't matter any.

MEAL NO. 2: LUNCH

"What the fuck you want me to do, Kenny?" Martha points her fat finger at him. I can hear her arm separate air. "Force feed her? You want me to go in there and shove food down her? She can't even chew for fuck's sake."

I can't hear the door close, but I can hear the key lock into place.

~

I can hear the crank of the sifter, and Martha bangs her hand against its cheap tin side. She is baking a cake. It isn't for me. It's only for her, always.

The chocolate goes into the microwave.

I count for thirty seconds and there is a buzz.

Martha cracks an egg, whisks it in.

The electric mixer comes alive and twirls; it spins.

Martha sets a timer but there's not a clock in my room.

When it chimes, she opens the oven door.

All I hear is chewing.

~

I'm getting hungry but it'll pass. After a while, I'll forget.

MEAL NO. 3: DINNER

"There's my girl." Here's Martha, in my room, talking just like Kenny.

I pretend I'm sleeping. My eyes are closed and the room is beginning to darken. It's night and I don't know where Kenny went.

Her feet drag heavy along the carpet.

"You awake?"

"No ma'am," I say, not knowing any better. I fall for it every time.

"You're so fucking dumb, just dumb as a plate, you hear me?"

She wheezes to my bed. My eyes are still closed but her shadow over me is large and black. It eats up all the light.

"I—" I wish I could take my hands and cover myself. It's cold now. I can't feel the cold but I know it's there, in her shadow, a looming wind, waiting to blast me with chills and fever.

She puts a pillow on top of my face. "There, there," Martha says. "Be a good little baby girl."

I don't struggle. I let her do it. I have no choice. "Take me," I say into the cheap cotton stuffing.

"Fuck you," Martha says. My face feels air. Everything is light again.

Martha stomps away.

MEAL NO. 4: DESSERT

I can hear the cardboard separate from its seal, and Martha takes scissors to the plastic bag. She is baking a cake. Of course it's for her.

Martha cracks an egg. She whisks it in.

The electric mixer comes alive, twirls: it spins.

Martha sets the timer. I don't need to count. I can feel time.

When it chimes, she opens the oven door.

All I hear is chewing.

~

I don't need hunger.

~

Because I can't feel a thing.

This is called luck.

Good fortune.

This is the prelude to my death.

FROM BEHIND, FROM BEYOND

Today, Martha dives into a dream full of delicious cake, marble and swirling. She surfs on waves of icing and falls into a gooey core of sweetness when her legs can no longer support the weight of gravity. This is the only kind of ocean she loves. She swims and blows bubbles. They wait there for her to bust them with her biting teeth.

~

Martha looks into the dirty mirror and sees somebody quite beautiful.

She snarls and the image becomes her own again.

~

Today, Martha calls her celly a Mexi-cunt, and when she gets stabbed in the arm, she throws the whole of her body into the girl. She is pinned to the cinder block wall.

Blood is slick magenta.

~

Today, there is only quiet. No one speaks to Martha and she says nothing either. Martha eats, employing silent mastications.

∼

Today, Martha takes a shower. I watch the cheap cotton struggle off her body, how she shivers but hides nothing. She stands as high as she can, proud of her mass, at what it has done.

She whistles while soaping and rinsing out her hair.

∼

Martha does not know how to miss Kenny. She tries but she can't remember a damn thing about him, not his hair, not his smile, not even his touch. He is even worse than a ghost: it's like he was never beside her at all.

∼

Today, Martha spits her meds out right in the guard's face. "Fuck you," she says. She tries to punch him, and her clenched fist hits the metal bar instead. It immediately swells and shadows rise from below the skin.

"Don't be like that, Martha," the guard says. "Just be a good girl."

He bends down and gathers her pills in his hand.

They make a chalk and saliva rainbow in his open palm.

∼

Martha yells out, "Arlene!" Her eyes are closed and even though the light in her cell is closed, the fluorescence from outside never turns off. It never dims. "Get your ass in here."

"Sorry," I say, but she can't hear me because I'm not really here. I'm here, but I'm not. I'm not real anymore.

I may have apologized, but inside, it feels like victory just happened for the very first time.

~

Today, Martha misses our old house. She misses her television. She misses her game shows and her dope operas. She laughs at her funny. "Dope," she says. "Dope dope dope." She even misses how the image would scramble sometimes and how happy she felt when it got fixed.

~

Today, Martha is reading a crime book and she wants to solve the case before the lawyer and the police and the reporters and everybody else, too.

She wants to be the best.

She wants to be the winner.

"I read that one already," her celly says. "Not too bad."

"Shut up," Martha says.

"Fuck you," her celly says. She says, "It's the mom. It's always the fucking woman who takes the blame."

Martha tears the book in half and throws it at her celly.

Her celly catapults it back, and the book bounces off of Martha's fat.

The pages fan and then they fall flat.

~

Today, they chain Martha's wrists and ankles to a post on the floor of a van. There are six other women with her, and she doesn't look at a single one of them.

Instead, she sings about beer bottles falling down from a wall and she stomps when each one crashes to the ground.

Martha could sure go for a margarita right now, no salt. The ice would cool her right down.

~

Martha brushes her teeth with her index finger because her toothbrush has been taken away from her. She lets the water pool in the cup of her hand and swallows instead of spits.

~

Today, Martha skims the last few pages and then she closes the book.

"Told you, didn't I?"

"It ain't right," Martha says.

"I know."

Her celly's hair is braided in plaits. Martha laughs, randomly and loudly, and starts to count on her fingers the many hours it would take her mama to untangle that head. 'Whammy!' she screams, pulling at her own hair.

"Ain't that just how the free world works?" her celly asks.

"Yeah," says Martha. "We always just go in here. Stay forever."

"Right?"

"Yeah," she says, and there is a small moment of understanding between these two women. There is something resembling sympathy, something like bonding—and then there's also disgust.

~

Today, Martha snores and her snores are robust. They boom.

~

Today, Martha licks an envelope and carefully writes her name and return address in the left hand corner.

She has her SID number memorized because she has been in here so long.

~

Martha leans into the shadow of a wall. She hates rec time, but the guards make her go.

It's hot, and there aren't any clouds up in the sky. Just the sun, low and tender.

~

Today, Martha writes a letter to a man in the free world who loves her, says he does at least. He promises her that he's going to see her soon, and she puts his name on the visitation list. What man could love her though? Only the three fools who came before, before she's set to get the cocktail. But there will be more, don't worry. There will always be more fools.

Martha can charm men, even beneath the barbed wire of prison, even when the day of her death is already scheduled on the calendar.

~

Today, Martha is starving. She is really, really hungry.

~

Today, Martha refuses to work because for her, there is no such thing as time off for good behavior. Wouldn't matter because she's always hated goody-goodies.

Her only goal is to continue everything she's already doing—until she can't do it anymore.

For her, hope has totally disappeared.

~

Today, Martha tries to order commissary, but she doesn't have any money on the books.

~

Today, Martha makes a long distance call to the free world.

She says, "You coming still?"

She says, "Daddy."

She says, "You promised me."

She says, "No, I love you more."

She holds the metal wire so hard her fingers sweat.

"No, me," she says, and she twists her foot around as if flirting.

She's not wearing any socks.

~

Today, Martha imagines she's a bird, kiting in the sky.

MARTHA, CONFINED

From my room, I can hear the television going, and I guess the thing about electricity is that it doesn't need to take a break. From my room, I can't tell if Martha is actually watching television all that time or if maybe she just leaves it on and goes and does something else, but I don't think Martha can do much of anything anymore, so it's most likely that she sits on that dirty couch with a stained sky blue sheet thrown over it and eats and eats and watches until she falls asleep and when she wakes up, the pattern continues on without disruption—whereas I must remain in my room. I can't move. My body stopped working, and it's been long enough that I can't remember what it might feel like to use my body to do something like, I don't know, run around. Or hug a friend. Or do anything at all. It's like I'm just my head now, except that the rest of my body is still there, this dead thing that's attached and won't let me go. I stink. Kenny changes my diaper for me every day, but that's only once. And it's first thing in the morning. So the first thing even though I haven't even had the time to poop yet. Every time Kenny opens the diaper, he jumps back and covers his nose with both his hands. I know he doesn't do it on purpose or anything. It's natural. This is how a body responds to disgust, and that disgust belongs to me.

It used to be that I would get embarrassed that Kenny was not just looking at but even touching me down there, but then we both knew that if he didn't, no one else would. We agreed that there was nothing to be ashamed about, that he was a grown man and I was already eleven and besides that he always thought of me as his daughter, nothing else.

Every time he gives me a sponge bath, he asks if the water is warm enough, because he could always heat it up some more. I can't feel a thing, not one single thing at all, but still, I say, "The water's perfect, Kenny. Just perfect."

"You're sure?"

"It feels really nice."

"And what about this?"

From how I'm laid down, I can't see Kenny's face, but I see the sponge making small circles by my ankles. "It's great. It's such a relief to feel clean again," I say to Kenny.

"I bet it does. What about this? How's that feel?"

I know he means good, but it's almost like he forgot that I'm paralyzed. Like, maybe he wants me to lie to him. "I like that a lot," I say.

"You promise?" Suddenly, Kenny's face is right up next to mine. I love that face. If there is any chance that I might escape Martha, it will be because of Kenny. I can't do it alone. I can't do anything alone. Kenny has to be the one to save me.

"Yes, Kenny," I say. I force him to keep eye contact with me for what feels like a very long time. "I promise you that it feels just the nicest. I promise you."

At the beginning, both me and Kenny were shy about it, but everything wears down over time, even humiliation and hope.

~

In my room, I am all alone for almost every minute of the day. In the mornings, Kenny comes in and changes my diaper and fills two plastic bags with nutrition, which slowly immerses itself into my body. I don't get hungry, but I miss the sensations of the mouth: the brightness of sour; how oatmeal turns from mush to a sloggy liquid; breaking open the skin of an apple and diving through its flesh; cherry chapstick; the leftover taste after flossing. I've never fantasized about food, but I still miss the act of chewing my food, letting liquid fill my mouth until I'm almost forced to spit it out but then I manage to swallow. I miss my first kiss, which I will never know, my lonely mouth, barren except for my own voice that only gets more and more inaudible from lack of use and practice.

In school, I learned that some people who get sent to prison and who are really terrible get put in a cell all by themselves and they don't ever go out of it except for maybe an hour or two per day and even then they aren't allowed to talk to anyone else. This is what my life feels like. I lay stuck in this bed all day and the best company I get is from the television out in the living room, where Martha is. I listen to the shows she watches. I hear her groan when she tries to get up or move around. It's hard for her now, harder than before I bet, because I can't help her. And she's lonely, too, I bet, because she can't yell at me or anyone else, really, because Kenny comes home late enough that I'm already sleeping and he wakes up before Martha to take care of me and then he leaves right away. Martha's still snoring when I hear the front door lock us both inside, together but very alone.

Most of the day, Martha talks to the television and sometimes she talks to Little Jimmy, too, even though he's dead. She never tries to talk to Suzie Ann or Erwin, or maybe she just doesn't call them out by name like she does with Little Jimmy. Sometimes I get so lonely in here I wish she'd come talk to me. I wouldn't even care if she wanted to scream at me or hit me or kill me. It wouldn't be so bad if she'd just kill me like she killed the others. I don't think so at least. Is it so strange to pray for your own murder? It's not like I know or anything, but I'm pretty sure that no matter how bad death is, it must be better than how I'm living now.

I wonder if Martha feels this way, too, and that's why she won't do it. She wants me to suffer. I want to tell Martha that I know she's suffering the same way I am. I want her to know that I understand the effects of isolation. I feel bad for her. I know she wanted to be a good mother to me, to all of us, but for some reason she couldn't do it. Or maybe it was an act of mercy. Maybe she knew that she's such a terrible mother that the most generous thing she could do was kill. So why won't she just do it? Get rid of me? She's always saying the house stinks of me. It's true. The whole house stinks, but I'm only physical smell. The real odor comes from the evil inside Martha.

⁓

"Morning, sugar," Kenny says. It's dark outside the window. "How you feeling today?"

"Same, I guess," I say.

Kenny checks all my bags and cleans me up the best he can.

"Kenny?"

"Yeah?"

"I don't want to live anymore."

"Arlene, you don't mean that."

"I do. I really do."

"The doctors say you can get better."

"That's not true."

"It is. I promise. I just talked to a specialist in El Paso yesterday. He has a new treatment he thinks will fix you right back up."

"Kenny, please? I can't do this anymore."

He reaches over and strokes my hair. He tickles me behind my ear and pulls out a quarter. He grins real big and I give him a chuckle, not because I mean it, but because I know he's trying to make me feel—I don't know what he's trying to make me feel. Hopeful? Happy? As if I would ever know those emotions again.

"Shut your goddamn traps in there. I'm trying to sleep!" Martha yells from somewhere else in the house.

Kenny makes a face like a baby who just got caught doing something it knows is wrong but is pretending like it didn't happen.

"Darling," he says, "I would do anything for you, you know that, right?"

The morning birds are beginning their shifts of song, welcoming the sun and trilling salutations to each other.

"Help me, Kenny, please?"

The pain kicks hard all over my body again.

"Arlene? You OK? Talk to me." He opens my mouth and puts three pills in and squeezes enough water in for me to swallow.

"Just give it a second, OK? You'll feel better in just a few minutes, I promise."

He's right. The pain gets smaller, but I know it'll come back ten times worse as soon as Kenny walks out that door, which he does, every single day, until the day that Martha kills me.

FROM BEHIND, FROM BEYOND

Today, Martha meets a psychologist and he makes her take a lot of tests. She is angry and confused.

Afterwards, he tells her she did just fine. He says, "There's a good—"

But I am gone before I can hear what else he says. When I return to my murdered ghosts, I am still crying.

~

Today, Martha sits on her bed, her bed that is just a mattress and its plastic protective cover and metal coils and in between the mattress and the coils are stacks of letters. Her face is serene and her eyes are vast. Today, she is scared. Nothing is ever good. Martha is nothing good at all. She deserves no good in her life—ever after.

~

Today, someone sends Martha a commissary package full of chocolate and this is what Martha calls love, this, right here.

She eats everything all at once.

There will be more to come. She knows this.

~

The doors open for rec time, and today, Martha goes out and doesn't make any fuss about it.

~

Martha has not seen the moon in years now, maybe a decade. Who knows.

She doesn't care though. It's not like she ever went out to look at it when she was in the free world.

~

Today, Martha sits on the steel toilet and grunts. She is glad she's not some skinny bitch who would just fall in because there's no seat on there. This doesn't make it any less cold on her skin.

~

"Daddy," Martha whines into the telephone.

"I know," she says.

She says, "But I can't wait anymore."

"I know," she says.

"Me too," she says.

"Aight," she says. "See you on Friday. I'm excited."

She says, "Promise?"

"No, promise me," she says.

She says, "Of course I do."

She says, "You know I do. More than anything."

"Don't you go teasing me now," she says.

I don't get to hear the other end, but that's not exactly something I want to hear, either.

~

Carlos says, "I want to marry you."

"For real?"

"Will you?"

"You're sure?"

"Of course I am."

Martha says, "I ain't never gonna be free."

"I know that," he says.

"Fuck's wrong with you?"

"I just love you mama," he says. "I love you so much. You're so special. I've never met—"

"Am I?"

"Course you are mama."

"I ain't some mama anymore," she says.

"That's no problem. I got plenty of my own."

"And they need a mama?"

"They do," Carlos says. "I need you too." He puts his hand against the plexiglass, and she puts hers up against it, too. "We need you."

The loudspeaker calls that visitation time is over.

~

Today, Martha steals her celly's cake and hides it in a safe spot so she can have it later. The cake gets smashed, but it will taste the same to her no matter what form it takes.

She sneaks a bite here and there, every time her celly turns her head.

~

Today, Martha bums a smoke. She hasn't had one in God knows how long, but she craves something, anything to make the time pass.

Time goes like time, never any faster, so she inhales and then she exhales, and it smells like nostalgia.

~

Today is Christmas so they serve turkey.

Martha goes, "Gobble gobble."

It doesn't have any flavor, and they never include salt with her tray.

~

Today, Martha's appeal gets denied, but don't worry, Martha, there will be others.

Soon enough you will be free.

I want her to die in prison.

But I can't make anything happen. Never could.

~

Today, Martha has a brand new celly, she says, "Why you here?"

"I don't want to talk about it," her celly says.

"Fucking bullshit," Martha says. "Everyone wants to talk about it."

"I don't."

"That bad?"

"Nah," she says, "it ain't."

"Then tell me."

"Ain't none your business." Her celly says, "You want to talk all big? What'd you do?"

"Nothing," Martha says.

"You a fucking liar is what you is."

"What?"

"I heard about you. You's a fucking baby killer."

"What?" Martha sounds surprised.

"You's a fucking baby killer."

"I—" Martha's bed is made. The sheets are tucked in real nice. "I only did what's right."

"You a goddamn evil bitch." Her celly pulls down her pants so she can take a piss.

~

Today, Martha is full of tears. She cleans her face with the sleeve of her shirt.

~

Today, Martha writes a letter, but her pen goes dry before she can finish. She presses down hard on the paper, using her might and her will. When she raises it up against the light, she can read what's written.

~

Today, Martha decides she should marry Carlos. There's no celebration. She just sits there like it's any other day.

~

Today, there's visitation, but the guards don't call her name.

~

Love stitches lilies around Martha's heart.

She hates flowers.

~

Today, Martha misses me. She misses Little Jimmy and Erwin, too.

~

Martha can neither see nor hear the monsoon outside, so it doesn't much matter to her.

~

Today, Martha kills two mosquitoes. They're stupid for coming in there, just to die.

MARTHA, IN LOVE

Already, the girl has fallen off the roof.

She waffles into and out of the hospital.

Girls are not as hardy as boys, they're more weakly constituted. Don't go telling any of the girls in there with Martha something like that, but this isn't about the girls in there. It's about girls before they become murderers and criminals, back when they're just girls, so innocent and vindictive that they radiate. Arlene used to shine.

~

Arlene is singing a song. Her voice is timid.

~

Its melody is almost familiar.

~

Martha put a plastic bag over her daughter's head.

~

A grocery bag curtain.

~

Condensation drips down the plastic canals, leaves stains of salt along her skin.

It is from Arlene's screaming. Her mouth just suctions in the plastic.

Plastic up her nose.

The gape of her mouth.

~

Martha throws the girl on the bed.

~

Who is this girl?

~

She looks like someone else.

~

She does not fight.

She is limp, a dump of weight to haul around.

The girl is bigger than a baby.

Martha looks at her.

This girl is almost familiar.

She adjusts the girl's head.

The plastic sounds like a herd of hippos against this backdrop of gravitas.

Or an ocean going wild. Throwing a party.

Martha feels tired now, so she sits down.

~

The night before, Kenny had said some terrible things.

He packed up his bags and left.

He might've taken Arlene with him, but she was in bed already. She is always in bed.

She can't move anymore. She can't fight.

He thinks she can't die, either.

He could have saved her life. Or at least delayed its end. He could have saved her life. It doesn't matter, not really.

An object moves in one direction: forward.

The continuation of movement.

Because I die, will die, am dead—for revenge, for desperation, this is Martha, in love.

FROM BEYOND

Once upon a time, a mother is weeping along the river. This is a song for Martha.

~~

Kenny sees you walking along the river. In the moonlight you were glowing like Venus.

~~

There are people who call me dark—a caring shadow of a girl. I am like the green chile: crust or whole I am still good.

~~

Alas, weeping Martha as tangerine as the setting sun, although I am not longer living. I cannot stop loving you my mother true.

~~

From the bend in the river, water flows and the flower is

born. If they ask you who is singing, tell them it is the desert in search of love.

⁓⁓

I climbed the Organ Mountains to look at you—the mountain was kind and wept when it saw how I was weeping.

⁓⁓

Each night comes, I begin to think, and I say, "What's the purpose of a bed if not to die, if not to never wake?"

⁓⁓

From the Gulf of Mexico and all the way across Texas, a letter sent by a mermaid, and in the letter she said, "Love is pain and pain and pain."

⁓⁓

Alas, take me to the Rio Grande and cover me with your body, because I am dying from all this cold.

⁓⁓

They say I don't have sorrow, because no one sees me crying. The dead do not make any noise, but our pain is grand.

⁓⁓

If I could climb up to the sky, I'd get the stars down for you. I'd put the moon at your feet and crown you with the sun.

~~

Alas, I am the weeping girl of yesterday and today and tomorrow all the same. Yesterday I was a wonder, but now I am not even a shadow left.

~~

Alas, weeping mother of darkness, with this one verse I say goodbye, worshipping you on my knees.

~~

I don't know what's in the flowers, the flowers of the cemetery, but everything seems to cry when the wind blows with its might.

~~

Alas, you are my mother. I can no longer love you, because I can never forgive you, because I can never forget.

~~

On an iron chair you were supposed to die. What could have been my pains relieved.

~~

Alas, weeping mother of the lily field. You do not know how to love, do not know how to sacrifice, either.

~~

Two kisses live forever inside my memory: the last one from my mother, and the first one I ever gave you.

~~

Alas, I am here in the place where love is forgotten and suffering begins.

~~

Lift your eyes to the night sky and see a star that weeps and sighs in regret: it is Venus setting, still so bright and bold.

~~

Alas! Weeping mother of yes or no, the light that once made me has left me here in shadows.

~~

They say that a mother's love is big and true, but a daughter's love is better and bigger than all.

~~

Alas, give me a star. Let me go and let me fly.

~~

Don't think that because I sing, Martha, that my heart is warm; I sing for pain, Martha, because all my weeping is done.

~~

Poor me, Martha, Martha give me your love. The sky can wait but I can't escape from you.

~~

I love you because I must, Martha. I love you because you are my mother.

~~

If you want me to love you more, I have already given you my life. What more do you want? How can you want more?

~~

Poor me, Martha. Yesterday I saw you weeping, Martha, under the fluorescent lights.

~~

Poor me, Martha, somehow I still love you so. You don't know that I love you, Martha, because you don't know how to weep.

~~

If because I love you, Martha, you want me to return to death, let that be, Martha, let me die again so that you too may die and this time die for me.

~~

Poor me, Martha, take me to the sky. I want to join the praying women, Martha, I want to join the sky.

~~

Alas, do not be this way, Martha. I beg you on my knees: remember me your daughter, remember what you have done.

~~

I have so much pain, Martha, that I can almost say I have no more pain at all. This is a pain that owns me, Martha, it never goes away.

~~

Poor me, Martha, let me weep to see if by weeping, Martha, my heart might learn to rest.

~~

When you go by our old house, Martha, the dirt you step on is hard and dry. No one walks there anymore, Martha, because you have not left a single one to live.

~~

Poor me, Martha, between two ways: how beautiful a kiss I've never kissed, Martha, a love I never could learn.

~~

A badly damaged heart, Martha, only with weeping rests.

The richness of death, Martha, because with you I was only naked hope.

~~

My mother is to blame, that's you Martha, by taking your body onto mine. The wind pushes out of me, Martha, for your body lies asleep.

~~

Poor me, Martha, Martha of cake and sadness. The cake is in your hands, Martha, and the sadness stays with me.

~~

If I leave I feel a pain, Martha, if I stay I feel two: I don't do either, Martha, I don't feel a thing. Not for you, Martha, this is song is no longer for you.

~~

This is a song of damnation, Martha. This is a song of sorrow, Martha. This song is the melody of my death, Martha. This is how I sing to rest.

ACKNOWLEDGMENTS

The author would like to thank the following people, groups of people, and institutions for their support—emotional, fiscal, literal—over the past fifteen years that it has taken for this novel to become: Kazim Ali; Melisa Bañales; Kate Bernheimer; Blake Butler; Joshua Cohen; Ben, Sandra, and Alphie Doller; Rikki Ducornet; Fredrik Farnstrom; Carmen Giménez Smith; Sabrina Gomez; Richard Greenfield; Scott Holcomb; Jac Jemc; Evan Lavender-Smith; Sarah Luna; Martha Millard; Townsend Montilla; Nell Pierce; Red Hen Press (especially Kate Gale! Thank you for taking a chance on this beastly novel!); Selah Saterstrom; Anna Joy Springer; Katie Jean Shinkle; Brandon Som; Jackie Wang; the English Department and MFA Program at New Mexico State University (especially my students!); NMSU College of Arts & Sciences; the Virginia Center for the Creative Arts; and the Department of Literature and MFA in Writing at UC San Diego (especially my students!).

The author would like to acknowledge the very real human on which this book is based. Her name is Martha.

And, finally, the author would like to thank her family, in particular her mothers and this matrilineage of suffering that reminds us that every small joy should be shared as victory.

BIOGRAPHICAL NOTE

Lily Hoang is the author of five books, including *A Bestiary* (finalist for a PEN USA Nonfiction Book Award) and *Changing* (recipient of a PEN Open Books Award). She has been a Mellon Fellow at Rhodes University in South Africa, a Distinguished Visiting Writer at Cornell College, and a Cultural Exchange Faculty Fellow at Wuhan University in China. To date, she has taught creative writing on five continents. She currently teaches in the MFA Program at UC San Diego. She lives in San Diego, California.